floating lines

*f*loating lines

Short Stories
by
Denis Baker

For Eric & Wynn

Best wishes,

Denis B.

DL

David Ling Publishing Limited
PO Box 34601, Birkenhead,
Auckland 10, New Zealand

Floating Lines
First Edition

Published with the assistance of a grant from

ISBN 0-908990-68-5

First published 2000

Typeset by Pages Literary Pursuits
Printed in New Zealand

'Chana says . . .' and 'This Sporting Life' were first published in
Metro. 'Getting Away From It All', 'Waiting for the Bell' and 'The
Perfect C', were first broadcast by Radio New Zealand. 'Neither
Sane nor Merely Dedicated' was published in *Penguin 25 New
Fiction*. 'Cool' first appeared in *Takahe*. 'Access' (published as 'Fish')
was runner-up in the 1998 *Sunday-Star Times* short story contest
and was later printed in that paper. A version of 'Panadeine' was
butchered by *Grace* magazine without approval and published
under a different title. 'I was Mr New Zealand *or* What Scares Me'
was second runner-up in the 1999 Takahe Short Story Award.

Contents

Acknowledgements

No collection is complete without thanking those who helped make it possible. And no matter who is listed there will always be a raft of others, unmentioned, who contributed in some way, the greatest sin of a thank you list being that of omission, but these are the people whose fingerprints are on the pages.

Steve Danby at National Radio for unfaltering support, expert guidance and brilliant rejection letters. Sarah Weir, David Brown and Veronica McLaughlin, sounding boards and critics at Kamo. Liz for her patience and for the use of Kawau. Lorenzo for Turangi.

Finally, and most importantly, my parents, for understanding what it means.

Access

There are days when my past surrounds me. As if it's sped up or I've slowed down and somehow we've collided. On those days, Elton John works in the store at the end of my road and my ex-wife lives right across the hall.

It's neither of them of course. Corner-shop Elton has got his own hair and the woman across the hall's never been married, doesn't have my kid, and isn't starting her life over. But there she is, true to life; the spitting image of Deirdre.

On those days the guy working in the bank looks like someone I used to drink with when I was younger, and the guy on the bus looks like a guy I once worked with in a kitchen. To top it all off there's a regular who's a doppelgänger for an old girlfriend from way back when. Not just her features, but everything; the way she moves, holds her head, laughs, even the way she stirs her drink. She's so similar I can look at her and feel I know her intimately. As though I've slept with her, even though I haven't.

A couple of times, like at the end of a long shift or on those days when I've had enough and my defences are down, I've almost fallen for her. It's not that hard. *Colpo di fulmine* the Italians call it. She'll come to the bar, do that thing with her hair the girlfriend used to do, maybe flash an innocuous little smile and I'll be lost. My stomach will flip and all those feelings will come flooding back better than a memory.

I won't fall of course. She's not the girlfriend and the wash of love I feel is old, not new. It's not even for her. It's a nostaglic love for another, perfected by time, cocooned in the past. I cannot have it over and only a fool would disturb it.

Still, I dream of the past.

Until I looked at it through his eyes, I'd never realised how small my room is — although I doubt he'd even notice. There's little chance it will happen, but in case we come back I've tidied up. Made sure there's no washing hanging about, vacuumed, made the single bed. The chair and dresser are free of junk. The hand basin in the corner now gleams, its stained porcelain like the worn dentures of an old salt. Above it the mirror is clean, if a bit rusty around the edges, and the whole place reeks of cleaner.

It was during the days I slept that the room really began to smell. Whole days, whole nights. Weeks of sleeping without rest, waking exhausted and turning to sleep again. Occasionally I would rouse myself, shower, attempt to face the world, but I always ended up back in the sack, knackered, unable to keep up the momentum.

I take a last look around the room, wish the walls were a different colour then shut the door and walk down the corridor. He won't be coming back here anyway.

The bus, as usual on weekends, is late. Walking down the aisle nobody looks like anyone I know and nobody recognises me, not that they should. I take a seat in the middle and wait. It's a long way back to the house. Five stages on the bus from home to home. The new to the old. I keep thinking it will get easier, but the next step always seems harder. God knows if the first time is this hard for everyone.

It's difficult to believe my sleeping days were the easiest, if the most bewildering. That kind of insidious sadness is exhausting, but in a merciful way. It depletes you, prevents you facing more as everything just shuts down. From the inside it feels like the end, like living is simply too hard and takes too much energy to be worth it, but really it's only the beginning. From there it just gets worse.

After the sadness, it's the guilt that really gets you. Leaves you curled around your emptiness, awake, alert, re-living the same horrifying moment like some mad highlights package until you either do something about it or just check out. But I was never going to let myself off that easy.

Perhaps, I should have bought them something. A toy, a game, some flowers maybe. It's too late now. All I have in my bag is a raincoat and a wallet with our lunch money.

The first thing I do off the bus is light a cigarette. Not that the cigarette itself is particularly calming, but the habit is, the familiarity. It's only once I've smoked it to the butt that I start walking. Purposefully. Along the road. Up the hill. Through the gate. Past the hanging plants that need watering.

Deirdre answers the door.

"Hi," she says. "You're early."

"Yeah, sorry," I say. "The driver was a maniac." Her hair is up and she has some make-up on, but apart from looking a bit tired, I can't read her. "Where's John?"

"Cleaning his teeth," she says.

"Oh." I shift my weight. She's wearing slippers.

"Come in," she says and I walk into our house.

"How are you?" she asks, walking into the living room.

"All right. How about you? Busy?"

"We're doing okay."

"That's good," I say. The cat flap rattles and Splotch crawls through. He lets out a cry and runs to me. I pick him up, put him over my shoulder and scratch his ears. He purrs loudly.

"Looks like someone still loves you," says Deirdre.

"Mmm," I say, more to the cat.

"Dad!" John pelts into the room, hits me at speed and Splotch leaps for safety.

"Hello Tiger." His arm goes tight around my neck, head pressed against my shoulder. I encircle his waist and stand up with him, my other hand on the back of his head. He smells freshly showered and my eyes fill. Deirdre is looking at the floor.

"Did you get the gear ready?" I ask. He doesn't answer, still hanging on. Deidre gives a little smile and I bend down and put his feet back on the ground. Reluctantly he releases his grasp. He's wearing patched-kneed trousers that stop at his ankles and a sweat-shirt with a hole under one armpit. The pink of the prosthetic arm and its stainless steel grabber sticks awkwardly out of his right sleeve.

"I put everything into the car already, Dad. Everything. You wanna see what Aunty gave me? It's a special bait-catcher and and . . ."

"Maybe you should put your shoes on John, get your jacket and you can tell Dad all about it in the car."

"But, but . . ."

"Go on," says Deidre, smiling. "If you don't get a move on, you'll miss the ferry."

John looks at her, then looks at me. I nod and he spins around and tears off to his bedroom. I follow Deirdre into the kitchen.

"I'd offer you tea, but . . ."

"No time," I say.

She adjusts a potted herb growing on the window sill, then fills up the kettle and plugs it in.

"He misses you."

"Yeah."

"Did you bring any food?"

I shake my head. "Just some money."

"Macdonald's is his favourite."

"I know, D."

"Of course, I didn't mean . . ."

"I know."

"Take this," she says. From the bench she hands me a thermos flask. "Milo. Keep you warm."

"Thanks."

"And these . . ." Two packages of loose biscuits wrapped in cling film from a shelf in the fridge.

"Thanks."

She swipes at something on the bench with a crumpled tea-towel. "He's really been looking forward to it."

"Me too."

"Will it be all right?" she asks.

"I can make it through a soap opera without crying, if that's what you mean."

"It's a start."

"It's a bloody triumph," I say and she laughs. The kettle boils and switches itself off. There's condensation on the window.

"Where are you going exactly?"

"Orakei Wharf."

"Be careful," she says, then her hand flies to her mouth. "God I'm sorry! I promised I wasn't going to say it. Really, I didn't mean it like that, I mean . . ."

"It's okay, D," I say. "It's okay."

She picks up the tea-towel and wraps it around her fist, stares at it.

"We'd better go. We'll miss the ferry."

"Yes," she says.

Outside, John has loaded our car, the car, Deirdre's car with every piece of fishing gear I own. Four boat rods, both surfcasters, a net, a gaff, three tackle boxes, his new bait-catcher, a fish container and the bait — which stinks.

"When did you load the car, John?"

"Yesterday," he says, brightly.

At least I know the bait won't be frozen. He climbs in and I turn to help him with the safety belt.

"I can do it," he says pushing me away with the arm, the steel cold against me. He struggles a little, but the belt clicks into place.

We pull out of the driveway, wave goodbye to Deirdre and head toward the ferry. Almost immediately spots of rain appear on the windscreen. Not enough to use the wipers, but a worry. Ahead the sky is grey, but the cloud high. We might be lucky. John is staring out the back window, waving madly to his Mum.

This the little man who followed me around, did what I did. Who mowed the lawns by pushing his plastic mower behind me, yelling at me over the roar about the bits of lawn he'd already done — but that might need another go. The little man I took to Saturday rugby, boots

11

awkward on young feet, who stumbled with the other kids in muddy glory and disappointment. The little man who later, in a different season, bowled twilight spin to me on the summer lawn.

It starts somewhere near my stomach and lodges in my throat, makes it hard to breathe. I swallow, bite my lip, *hard*, use every ounce of strength to keep it from reaching my eyes. I refuse to let it happen. I'm past all that, bursting into tears at the disaster of an undone shoelace. I am stronger now. I teeter on the edge, fighting until finally it begins to fall away, my throat slowly deconstricting. I breathe slowly. It's always there, just below the surface.

I reach across and with my fingers comb the wisps of sandy hair out of his eyes. He smiles and shakes his head, pushing it into the palm of my hand.

"Now, what about this bait-catcher?" I say.

In the ferry car park I do a quick run through of the fishing gear and decide what to take. A surfcaster and John's boat rod, the smallest tackle box and of course, the new bait-catcher which can carry the bait. John insists we take the net.

Suitably loaded down we get our tickets and John runs to sit outside.

"What's the biggest fish you've ever caught, Dad? How many can we take home?"

His voice is loud and eager. An elderly couple look up and immediately I see the pity spread across her face. She catches me looking and I turn away. Eventually everyone will look at the poor little boy with the plastic arm. After that they'll look at me, and then, even though I understand that it's not possible for them to, that rationally I appreciate it's not even true, I know they will look at me and know. Something will tell them and they will look at me with the cold eyes of fish, singular and accusatory.

"How *many*, Dad?" His eyes are wide.

"As many as we like."

"Really?"

"Yep."

"Cool. I'm gonna to catch ten... no, eleven, because that's five for you and five for Mum and one for Mrs Marshall."

Mrs Marshall is the baby-sitter Deidre employs for the hours after school.

"And what about me?"

"You're gonna catch eleven, too."

The wharf is different from what I remember. It has been shortened and most of the old planking has been replaced. There are so many people fishing I wonder if we'll be able to find a place.

"Look Dad!"

John is standing over a large bloody hunk of flesh. As I get closer I see it's a stingray, freshly caught, spread across the wharf inert and butchered. The sight of it sickens me. Why anyone would land it is beyond me. Apart from the danger of the thrashing tail, it's essentially useless. There is better bait. The tail of this fish has been hacked out and one wing roughly amputated. Blood, pooled around it's body, still oozes from the wound. In the water these are elegant, graceful creatures swimming in slow motion like shadowy marine bombers. Here it is an oddity.

"It's a stingray," I say.

"Wow," he says quietly.

"Come on," I say, and lead him away to the neck of the wharf where nobody is fishing.

"Is this a good place?"

"The best," I say.

We start him fishing. First the bait-catcher, filled with bread, securely tied and lowered into the water, then his rod. By the time I've put his rod together he's checked the bait-catcher half a dozen times.

"It's not working," he complains.

"Not up here it isn't," I say. "You have to forget about it, otherwise the fish won't swim in."

"Really?"

"Yep. And you have to whistle before you bring it up."

13

"Dad!"

"Honest."

I give him the rod, help him grab it with the steel claw, steady the butt in his belly and remind him how to work the star drag with his good hand. The first time he's impatient and lets the line go too quickly causing a snarl in the reel. It takes me five minutes to untangle it and the second time he's penitent and overly cautious.

"Is that right, Dad? Is that right?"

"That's great, John," I tell him.

I assemble the surfcaster and heave a long cast out into the blue. It's mostly for John. There's not that much around anymore for a rod like this.

As soon as the rod's set out I break into the Milo and biscuits, keeping one of Deidre's packets in reserve. My hands are already fishy from the bait and John takes his from cling film. We dangle our feet over the edge of the wharf and sit watching rod tips. He peers down to the bait-catcher and the small fish milling around it.

"Are you better now, Dad?" he asks me suddenly.

It takes me a second to answer. "I think so," says my voice.

"That's good," he says sagely.

God knows what conversations he's had or overheard. I fumble for a cigarette and wait for more, like the 'when are you coming home' I'm half expecting, but that's all there is. Instead he launches into a description of some new thing that might be a toy, a computer game, a tv show or maybe all three and that's when the fish strikes. The rod tip bending almost double and John letting out a cry.

"Loosen the drag, John, loosen the drag! Let him run or you'll lose him!"

The slim rod is bucking wildy, the rubber grip loose in the steel grabber of his plastic arm and I can see he's going to drop it.

"The drag, John!" but he can't do it. I reach around from behind him, take hold of the butt and release the tension. The fish runs a short distance and then as quickly as it arrived, we have it under control.

While I hold the rod steady, John plays the fish awkwardly, unused

14

to reeling with his left hand. The grabber clatters uselessly against the fibreglass of the rod. When we get it close enough, John insists we net it and then there, on the boards of the old wharf is a flapping shining snapper, all three pounds of it. The light bouncing rainbows off its scales.

"Not bad, John," I say, "not bad. Won't Mum be surprised?" He has his back to me, feet still hanging over the edge. I place a hand over the fish's head and with some difficulty work the hook loose.

"Good job, John."

He doesn't answer. Head down his shoulders are hunched. The rod dangles from the steel jaws as he sobs and begins slapping at the plastic arm.

I extract the rod from the jaws, then put my arms around him. He sobs, and I am in the past. I see my lathe, hear the telephone and again make the split-second decision to let it spin. With the telephone to my ear I see his arm stretch toward the spinning wood, feel the pit of powerlessnesss open as his sleeve catches and I watch him jerk forward.

We stay holding each other until he stops crying. I wipe his eyes and we drink Milo. Later, we check the bait-catcher, retrieve the prize. He laughs happily. Only when he sits, feet dangling, trying again, do I think about cleaning his fish.

The knife slips easily into the soft white belly and as I slide it forward toward the head, opening the fish up, that day in our shed is with me again. I push my hand into the cavity feeling for the guts, tighten my grip and pull. With a jerk they tear loose. I drag them out and throw them over my shoulder to the gulls.

I reach in again, but this time, with my other hand, cover the fish's head. I can't stand him looking.

This Sporting Life

"Sew-mate," he said, the Australian accent dancing across the words, "I actually thought I had the debut ton in the bag. I'd spent a coupla hours at the crease getting me eye in and finally things were beginning to open up. To be honest, mate, she'd looked fairly promising right from the start. Never a hint of hostility in the bowling, just gentle medium pacers on a good wicket with a sympathetic outfield. Everything a batsman needs Smithy — but you know me mate — never one to leap to any conclusions about the opposition's intentions. I took me time, got through that awkward early stage, and that's when it began to look good — deliveries just begging to be hit. Cripes, I fair raced to forty. Anyway, I'm on forty-five, convinced I'm looking a ton in the eye, preparing to collect the glories of the fifty and suddenly — down comes the bloody googlie! Out of nowhere! Jeeesus, mate! — middle and off all over the place. I couldn't believe it. One minute I'm flashing the willow with poise and authority, the next I'm on me way. I'll tell you Smithy, it was a bloody long walk back to that pavillion, mate, a bloody long walk!"

We were setting up the boat for that night's race and Minty wasn't talking about cricket. It was a competely different ball game he was discussing.

"Boyfriend?" I venture.

"Na, it was a bloody fiance! She slipped it into the conversation just before I made the move. Wouldn't it rip yer nightie?"

"Bummer," I said. "You're so unlucky."

"Well, mate, I dunno if it's luck or not, you know. Things have gotta get better soon, I haven't had a decent bloody innings for ages."

"What about last weekend? Didn't you have a fairly successful one dayer?"

"A quick fifty, mate and that was it. Ran out of overs and had that familiar walk back to the showers for a bit of batting practice."

There are, in my opinion, two types of ex-pats. Those who mix with others of like nationality and those who don't. I've always been one of those who didn't. I figured if I'd wanted all my friends to be Kiwis I would have stayed in New Zealand and not moved to Los Angeles, and I know Minty was the same. Anyway Minty was Australian, and that didn't count.

The day he arrived on the scene I was pinning up a 'Crew Wanted' notice at a Marina del Rey yacht club and he was standing by the board. We got into the standard kind of conversation the new imports like to have and I always try to avoid — about how long I'd been there and why — and I gave him my standard answer. (Four years; because I was sick of the wet winters and the weak dollar and being tucked away at the arse-end of the world three years behind everybody else.)

It was a conversation I'd had a million times before with other dreamers who thought they were about to get rich simply by turning up, and I was just about to move on when he asked me about the crew spot. I asked him if he'd done much yacht racing and instead of giving me the big pitch, said laconically, "Oh yeah. A bit," and I knew immediately what he meant.

We spoke some more and I knew we had to have him on board. It turned out he had more sailing experience than the rest of our crew put together — without including the round-the-world race. I gave him the information, tossed the notice in the bin and arranged to meet him the next Wednesday on the pier.

Crewing Wednesday night beer-can races on a forty-eight foot ex-TransPac yacht was my social, competitive and alcoholic escape from the pressures of selling real-estate by day and attending law school at night. Exactly what I needed for my relaxation, it was a way to see the boys and have a bit of a race without being overly serious — it wasn't called beer-can racing for nothing. But as soon as Minty came on board, all that changed.

He was a master tactician and helmsman who took it upon himself to get the boat moving as fast as possible as often as possible. The man's work rate was incredible, an inspiration to us all. Pretty soon the lackadaisical part of relaxation disappeared and he had us pushing that boat like it was the America's Cup. No one minded because he was so damn good — in fact, better than good. Before we knew it we'd started winning and were having more fun than ever before.

The boat's owner was a rich plastic surgeon who wanted to play at yacht racing, but had little desire to get wet and often didn't bother to show up — which was fine by us. Me, Minty, an Englishman named James, and Todd, a Californian, were the regulars and the only ones who actually loved sailing and racing. The other guys were what we called rail-bait, friends of the owner who didn't know a halyard from a cleat and changed almost weekly. Invariably we shoved them onto the rail with a beer in their hands, and let them hang their toes over the edge, while we raced the boat.

I think that's why Minty starting using 'cricket-speak'. So that he and I could have a relatively exclusive conversation without being blatantly rude to those around us. And generally, I think they found it quite amusing.

To achieve fluency you needed to demonstrate some understanding of the nuances of cricket, not merely go by some of the more obvious clichés, and the other guys just weren't able to do it. Besides, Minty's rules were quite malleable; what was orgasmic one day might only be foreplay the next, so you really had to know cricket to participate.

The only person who understood us properly was James, the Englishman, but he was an older, fairly serious lawyer with little time for the antipodeans and their ridiculous sullying of his national game. He was one of the 'other' ex-pats. The type that still love their country and spend the majority of their time denigrating their adopted home while enjoying the sunshine. He was a nice guy and we got on well, but we were not of his ilk. So it was left up to Minty and I to debate future scoring opportunities and decry the poor state of the wickets we were forced to play on.

For my part it was all talk. I was happy cohabiting with Rosa in our Venice Beach apartment and had neither the time nor the inclination to be out on the prowl with someone like Minty.

Still, he was a lot of fun. When he started talking cricket-speak, his accent became much broader, a parody of himself as an Australian if you like, and with the accent his whole demeanour changed. As he became increasingly animated his intonation would rock from consonant to consonant, and his walrus moustache would quiver furiously as if threatening to jump onto the deck and continue the gesticulations itself. It was a great sight and he single-handedly took the whole art of post-match analysis to a new level. And that's exactly what meeting women was to Minty, not merely a game, but a contest with a very real opposition and a great victory at stake.

Generally it all went well for Minty. He had the boat flying and we were winning the series comfortably, beating boats we wouldn't have dreamed of beating a few months earlier. He was rubbling off on everyone and when two of the owner's friends, Chuck and Vic, got serious and joined us as regulars, no one was surprised.

Meanwhile, I helped him find a live-aboard in the Marina, staying rent-free on a boat in exchange for maintenance work, while he got an under-the-table job cleaning boat hulls. The only problem with the job was that the boats were still afloat and he was spending eight hours a day in a wet suit and dive gear under the cold, faecal waters of the Marina scrubbing away at whatever lurgy grew.

It was one of the only decent money jobs he could get and he accepted it had to be done while he was finding his feet. At least it kept him close to the Marina, a good place to make contacts, but frequently he swore he could taste the water hours later, regardless of mouth-washes or preventative chewing gums, and lived in constant fear the smell would permeate his skin for good.

"It'd be the end of me career as a first-class batsman if it does," he worried. "Mind you, I'm not exactly performing brilliantly at the moment anyway, am I?"

And this seemed to be his only problem. It wasn't major, but it was a concern. Already it appeared that he'd decided to stay in LA — how he'd do that was none of my business and it's a question ex-pats rarely ask each other — but if he was going to stay, he at least wanted some female companionship.

LA's a big place, and the bigger the city, the lonelier a person feels, especially if you don't quite belong. It was paradoxical really. He'd had enough of Australia, but he needed an identity in this novel environment, something reassuringly familar and cricket-speak gave it to him.

"She's still looking a bit shabby, mate. A couple more low scores and I'll be spending more time practicing on me own in the nets than I will in the field."

And as his sole interlocutor and friend, it was my job to keep his identity secure until he did find his place.

"How's the average Minty?"

"Deadly mate, deadly. Got stumped badly on Saturday night."

"Her team-mate?"

"Yeah. He turned up with the drinks and there I was well out of me crease with his girlfriend."

"Night, night nursie."

"Abso-bloody-lutely."

In the end, I decided to go out with him and try to provide a little technical advice — if I could. I was crazy with work and school, but the boat was winning and I wanted to help him out.

To tell the truth, I couldn't understand how he'd performed so dismally. Here was an entertaining and intelligent man somewhere between twenty-five and thirty. He wasn't ugly, or particularly brash, wasn't fat or too short or overly tall. He wasn't in debt and came with an accent that had usually been the focal point for at least the start of a conversation in the seething pit of Marina bars.

We hit the town after racing one Wednesday night and it only took about an hour before I figured out what was happening.

"You know what you're problem is, don't you Minty? You've been playing too many one-day matches at home. You've gone international only to discover that your whole test match form has dissolved in a series of rash, hurried shots. You need to spend a bit of time on zero before even thinking about getting off the mark. You've got to adjust to the wicket."

"Are you saying I'm desperate?"

"In short? Yes."

"But I don't want to be in a test match," he protested. "Long-term is not what I'm after. I'm interested in the average. Fiftes and hundreds, and the possibility of a triangular tournament."

"It's attitude, Minty. Try it. At least think in terms of a three-dayer."

"Yeah, all right." he promised. "I'll give anything a crack once."

He never got the chance. About a week later on the following Tuesday afternoon, the Immigration and Naturalisation Service swooped on a corner of the Marina combing the boatyards for illegals, searching the pontoons with an almost military precision. Minty was right in the middle of it. It was the first raid at the Marina anyone could remember in a long time and they got more people than they could handle.

The first I heard about it was at the boat the next day. When I arrived Todd, instead of setting up, was sitting lethargically on the bow waiting for Minty, but he never showed up. Presuming the worst, we were gutted. That night James wanted to go out and race, but neither Todd or I, nor the other guys had it in us. We just sat in the cockpit drinking beer and feeling morose until it was time to go home.

It was over and we knew it. I'd lost a mate and our season was in tatters. Sure our lead in the series was unassailable, but without our star tactician it wasn't the same. In the following weeks we took the boat out, but our hearts weren't in it. Our teamwork was poor and without Minty we just didn't have the tactical know-how to remain competitive. After three weeks we had a boat meeting and decided that the next week would be the last.

⊰⊱

That final evening was the longest we'd ever taken to get the boat ready for racing. We were just about to push off, dangerously close to missing the starting gun, when a couple came running down the pontoon, the woman yelling at us to wait. At first I didn't recognise Minty. He'd shaved his moustache, had a baseball cap pulled low over his eyes and to my unsuspecting mind, looked typically American. But as soon as he opened his mouth, I knew.

"You pommy bastard," he yelled jumping aboard. "I'm sorry about ya wife running off like that mate, but there's no need to take it out on every bloody Australian that comes your way." James was backing up trying to keep the mast between him and Minty, but Minty was too quick for him. He grabbed him by the jacket, frogged-marched him to the stern and pushed him into the putrid Marina water, throwing one of the boat's life-preservers in after him. The woman, standing on the pontoon, applauded wildly.

"It was that little beggar that tipped off the INS," Minty said.

"Really?" I said half-heartedly. I was a bit stunned and for a second couldn't decide which was the greater shock; Minty turning up and tossing James in the drink, or Minty turning up with an absolute stunner who was now waiting for him on the dock. The other guys were having the same problem. I opted for the dock and turned to see her standing awkwardly, gazing about feigning nonchalance while waiting to be introduced, but knowing everyone was looking. Minty was busy watching James climb out of the water on the opposite pontoon. I cleared my throat at Minty and rolled my eyes in the direction of the woman.

"Oh sorry, luv," he said, remembering. "Fellas, this is . . . ah . . . Mrs Minty, Max. Max, these are the boys."

"Hi," she said.

"Hey," said Todd, California-casual as anything. I just nodded and smiled, completely unable to speak.

For a minute everything was quiet, just the sound of halyards rattling against masts and the distant squelching of James slinking off in the direction of the car park.

"Right," Minty said suddenly. "Now that we've got that over with, d'you slackers wanta race or not?"

We pushed off and motored up the channel to join the race fleet with Max on board. It wasn't until she went below that I had the opportunity to ask.

"Mrs Minty?" I was incredulous. "Immigration aren't going to buy that."

" ' course they will," he said.

"How do you know?"

"Because she works for them, mate," he said grinning.

"You sly bugger. So that's how you got your green card."

"Green card? What do I need a green card for? I got one of them before I came here — won it in the lottery."

"So what's going on?"

"I got married."

"You what!?"

"Smithy, y'know what you're problem is, mate? You're still playing like you were in New Zealand. You've gotta learn to adjust, mate."

"So what's the story?"

"No story, mate. I got arrested, met her, got released, went out, went to Vegas, got married, had a honeymoon. It's all very normal, Smithy. Very American."

"But what are you doing in a test match, Minty? You hate the very idea of them."

"I did, mate, I did. But I don't now. Now I'm playing for a draw, Smithy . . . I'm playing for a draw."

Neither Sane Nor Merely Dedicated

It was just like him. Only my father would be out on a morning snap frozen by winter. The sane would be in bed asleep, the dedicated waiting for the sun to break the icy grip, but my father, being neither sane nor merely dedicated, would be fishing.

It was the same when I was a child. I'd wake and search the house calling his name ready to perform my ritual assault of his waist, but instead of the welcoming safety of his arms and the warmth of his smell, I'd find the evidence left like a note. An essay in a half-finished cup of lukewarm tea.

This morning he would have left before dawn. I can imagine him sliding Long Johns over arthritic joints and building on them with layers of wool until he was wrapped like a mummy, desperately trying to ignore the pleas of his dodgy prostate. If they'd included the ten-metre shuffle — kitchen to toilet division — as an event at the World Masters games, my father would have won. He trained every morning. All he had to do was run water for the kettle and he was off — but not when he was bound by an impenetrable fortress of cloth. Not when there was fishing to be done. It was a recipe for disaster, and in the last two weeks I had discovered he was more than willing to accept the consequences.

It's more of a struggle for me. I drag myself out of bed, pull on the old tartan dressing-gown and pad out to the kitchen.

The dressing-gown had been mine as a teenager, but they'd never thrown it away. Instead, it had hung in the wardrobe like a talisman that might hasten my return, whiling away the time next to an old school blazer, various discarded shirts and some of my mother's ancient coats.

Wearing it is a regression, like being a child again, but so was everything else here.

From the minute I stepped inside the house, it was as if I had stepped back in time. Seventeen years after I left, most things are the same. Not just the rooms and the decor and the smell, but the rituals too. Everything is foreign yet intimately familiar. There is the same order for washing the dishes as there was in my youth and all the keys are still kept inside the pantry door. I feel dispossessed by it, as if my past is merely a dream. And it doesn't help that my father, oblivious to the fact that I am thirty-seven and have a ten-year old son of my own, treats me like the child I once was; or that I, trapped by the past, respond accordingly.

This morning is no different. I am again dressed as that child, wear his dressing-gown and once more am searching for him. At least the slippers are my own.

I find his empty teacup and to my surprise, utter one of his clichés. I'm not impressed. 'Creatures of habit' is my father's description for our family and it's not like me to agree with him. We're either that, I thought, or a human example of the repetitive behaviours you see at the zoo; caged animals slowly going insane.

The old tea is still hot in the pot, but I tip it out anyway and brew a new pot. He can't chew steak, thinks the floral designs on his crockery are part of the salad, but can spot a stewed cup of tea at twenty paces. It isn't worth the risk; stale tea would only upset him and that is to be avoided at all cost.

Fishing has always been my father's sanctuary. A retreat into calm from the pressures of the world around him. As my mother once wrote however, as if by explanation in those early years when we still corresponded at intervals more regular than Christmas, it is not a retreat of dedication, but of desperation. He loves fishing, no matter how unsuccessful. Never has it been about catching fish to him. Instead, it is the ultimate act of removal. Fishing is, and always has been, his way of dealing with a world in which he felt, for the most part, ill at ease. Thus whenever he had the opportunity, he would spirit himself away and stay away, undisturbed in a world that was entirely his own. A world where wives and children were not invited.

This was something I learned repeatedly as I child. That while fishing, father was not to be disturbed. Right through my childhood and teenage years, I observed the rule absolutely, but now, time and events conspire against us. It's not practical for a man of his age to be out alone in this weather.

On the first morning of my return, when I woke in the house and again heard his footsteps scratching down the hall, I'd swallowed the past's painful exclusion, risen and sat with him while he fished. I felt ridiculous, as if I'd achieved some ill-defined coming of age. As if I'd taken my place at a position I didn't want. We didn't say a word for three hours. In the middle of it I made tea and bought some toast, but he didn't eat. The rod never moved. I left him once the sun reached him, unsure whether I'd done the right thing. But later, small things suggested he had enjoyed my silent presence.

I re-wrap the dressing gown tightly about me and, clasping two mugs in one hand to open the door, step out into the cold to join him.

A thick layer of frost covers the morning and I shiver involuntarily. Placing a mug of tea on the table beside him, I sit in the other arm-chair and huddle around my own mug. He doesn't stir. He looks cold and elderly, and frost has formed on the hairy wool of his mittens. I didn't I realise how long he'd been there. Only the keenest, or most desperate of fishermen would put themselves through this.

The tea steams thickly, refusing to dissipate as if adding to the early morning fog that lies around us, dripping off trees and power lines, obscuring the city skyline. Apart from the occasional car driving past, everything is silent. I stare into the fog willing it to lift, waiting to see what it will reveal. Mother told me as a child that fog was God cleaning and if I looked hard enough afterwards, I would always discover something new.

Perhaps that's where my eye for detail comes from. I grew up watching this view of the city changing; watching motorways spread like snakes in the gully below the house, seeing buildings of ever-increasing aspirations stab at the distant sky. From this very spot I watched my father's back disappear lethargically up the hill on his way to work, and heard his unhurried footsteps echo toward me on his return.

In many ways I was a lucky child. Never did I think he would leave me alone on this verandah. Never did it occur to me that he might not return.

Of course, the first time I came home from school and found him fishing from our verandah remains fresh in my mind. Then I did not consider myself lucky. From then on I knew, beyond all doubt, that my family was different. Up to that point I had assumed it was merely school-boy paranoia — everyone at that age thinks their family is the odd one out, but that day I knew. Because of my father, we were different. He fished from the verandah of our house, and I was scarred by it.

In his working life my father had been an accountant, but one from the wrong age. He'd caught the bus at exactly the same time every morning and took it home at exactly the same time every night. He always wore an out-of-date, slightly ill-fitting charcoal suit and carried the same tired briefcase he had carried for the past thirty years. A man who worked solely for his family and his retirement, he was a backroom boy of the school overtaken by the world of corporatisation and high flyers. A man whose way of life had been made obsolete by those who could make three plus two equal whatever you wanted.

When his world began to change, and the procedures of the past that he had set his life by were thrown out, he was unable to adapt. My father enjoyed predictability. He had grown accustomed to an order of things in his life. Without it, he began smoking again and was unable to sleep. He began to withdraw, fishing more often — the real kind — at weekends and on long summer evenings, leaving earlier and returning later. It was about then that I, too young to understand but old enough to realise, lost my father.

The afternoon I discovered him fishing from the house was also the last day he would come home from work. I'd walked up the stairs to find him leaning back in the armchair with the rod held gently in one hand, his stare fixed intently on its tip. The butt rested across his thighs and his index finger was curled expectantly around the unhooked line that dangled, weighted, almost to the concrete bottom of the driveway below. A cigarette burned between the fingers of his left hand. I was seven.

That day, everything he had worked for, everything that he understood to be true had been proven false. He might have dealt with changing times at the office long enough to retire, but they couldn't deal with him. They'd loaded work on him, provided contradictory instructions, demanded more than was necessary of someone of such little importance and finally that day, instructed him to fire friends, colleagues. Rationalisation was a new way of thinking, one he was unable to do. The withdrawl was complete. Already weakened he shut down, emotionally, psychologically. From then on I think, my mother did everything. He became helpless without her.

On many occasions during my youth I came home to find him on the verandah, rod in hand. Yes, there were long periods when he didn't, but inevitably the day would come when he felt the need. It was his last resort when life became so heavy that he was unable to leave the house and fish for real.

I hated the action more than I hated him, although then, the two were synonymous. As soon as I was old enough I left, determined to do everything in my power not to be like the model he had made. But time passes. The fog lifts. I don't despise his imaginary fishing anymore, in fact I envy him. At least over the years he has succeeded. He knew what he needed.

Maybe I'm surprised to have found my father. Certainly my childhood and adolescence were both frustrating and fruitless — for all my searching he never looked for me. Instead he hid from the world and I fostered more than a fair share of resentment and contempt. Planning never to return I nurtured my anger for longer than I should have, but in the light of adulthood, it all eventually faded.

Sometimes I would like to know if it was one particular occurence that extinguished the rage. Whether it was the birth of my son or my marriage or my divorce, or simply the single event of growing older. I can't tell. Whatever or whenever it might have been, all I know is that I have found him. And for that, however unsatisfactory it may be, I am grateful.

He still holds the rod in exactly the way I remember. By now, wary postmen, sniggering newspaper deliverers and even the local dogs know to avoid the sinker that lurks at knee height. He is an unlikely neighbourhood legend.

Looking at him, I realise we are sitting the same. My legs are crossed as his, my shoulders, slumped and slightly rounded even in this chair, are his. Our hands are the same. It still disturbs me, because I can't help but wonder whether I am looking at my future.

Often my mother's letters would exclaim how I was never far away from her because she could see me in my father. From my fortress of self-exile I would frown vowing fervently to be me, chastising myself when I heard my father's tone in my own. I did not want to be the father's son my mother suggested I was, although the die was cast.

When I left, trying to escape what I despised, I did everything I could not to be him, but it was his flight I emulated. Over the years I thought I'd succeeded in exorcising him, only to return and find that I had not. Not only are we are physically similar, but I use clichés as he did and now, in this house when I scold my son, it is his voice I hear. I am resigned to the fact we are destined to carry our parents with us. My mother would have been proud. I'm not so sure. Pretend fishing is not how I want my son to remember me. I don't have my father's reasons.

Every morning since the day I arrived, I've watched him sit with his rod clasped in his hands, barely moving, occasionally drinking his tea, seldom touching the sandwiches I bring for his lunch. It is as if he hopes to catch her before she goes completely, hopes to drag her back to his world. Yet he knows all hope is lost. No trace or filament or vain cast into the void will bring her back. Age has won the fight, and as a result his distance is greater than ever.

"Morning Dad," I say to him brightly, hoping for the first time to break the spell, but as usual he doesn't reply. He is elsewhere.

If I could, I would reach into his secret fishing spot, throw my arms around his waist, and for a minute, an instant, drag him back to me. There is much I would like to say to him. Everything from the facetiously obvious, *How's the fishing?* to what I've wanted to ask since returning; *Are you all right?* There is no point in speaking those words now. They fall on deaf ears. Even if he wasn't an octogenarian with an aural tract full of nothing but the sound of rushing rivers, he wouldn't listen.

Still there is so much to say. I want to tell him that I never let go, that once I'd shaken the hooks of youth, I'd understood. I want to say that I too have felt the overwhelming weight of life that crushed him; to tell him that he was unlucky. That he was more than he thought, to me especially.

I want to say the words that will let him acknowledge the things I know he knows about us, because if it's true and I am my father's son, there is nothing for me to say. We know, we understand each other implicitly.

Instead of speaking, I sit quietly and watch his frozen form. The city has not woken. The air between us is calm, the tip of the rod, still. His heart, as inert as a block of ice, finally at peace.

I can't decide who I should telephone.

From inside the house as if from a long way away, I hear my son calling, looking for me.

Getting Away From It All

When your best mate is married in that all consuming way — to his wife, his job, his mortgage — it's hard to get the kind of quality fishing time you might like. That's the problem with being incarcerated in the prison of the daily grind. Plenty of intention, plenty of desire, but very little action. The only way Phil and I could get fishing was to agree on a day more than six weeks in the future when nothing would stand in our way. No lawns, painting, wall-papering, sanding, building, trimming, or visiting cousins-twice-removed for lunch. No spousal duty or got-to-get-it-done-by-Monday weekend work. Nothing. We'd consulted well in advance and booked the day. Crossed the damn thing off the calendar and waited with the kind of eager, optimistic patience only fishermen possess.

It would be twelve hours reduced to the barest essentials; the boys, the rods, the river and the fish. Large fish. Fresh-run rainbows that fight like Tyson in a corner. Fish that lurk at the very bottom of the coldest, darkest pools and know the difference between a well-presented Hare and Copper, and a hurriedly tossed Glo-bug. It was our day, and we'd looked forward to it like lifers to a parole. As Phil said, it was about getting away from it all.

Unable to leave the night before, I picked Phil up at four-thirty in the morning and we set off on the drive to Taupo hoping to arrive in time to catch the end of the morning's fishing. Phil had looked tired and muttered something about dinner parties, red wine and people who never leave, but threw his gear in the car with passion and urged me on as if his life depended on it.

All the way down we planned, compared new nymphs and talked

31

strategy; favourite rivers, specific pools and never-fail secret spots. We told each other stories of past conquests; fish we'd stalked with the stealth of warriors; perfectly weighted casts we'd floated millimetres from clutching ferns and dropped into fast moving water that swung the lure under tangled banks, swept it over stony lips and into the waiting mouths of trophy fish.

We knew we were going to get fish. It was just a matter of how many and how soon.

In the car we listened to the trout report, and even though it was a river neither of us knew and meant extra driving, excited details of the biggest fresh run seen in years convinced us it was the place to go. The report said the lower pools were holding the fish, but our combined wisdom at about seven that morning agreed the fish would have made it to the middle and upper reaches overnight. I suggested we take the four wheel drive to the middle reaches, walk up the rest of the way and fish our way down. Phil didn't argue.

At twenty past eleven, deep in the shadow cast by damp sandstone cliffs, I was up to my hip in river watching ice form in the eyes of the rod for the umpteenth time that morning, vaguely concerned about the lack of feeling in my fingers. My feet were frozen into painful blocks by water leaking through the previously undiscovered hole in my waders, and the bird's nest I'd created in my line roll-casting resolutely denied my icy fingers any solution. I'd already lost two sets of nymphs on snags and had managed this tangle trying to avoid the submerged log I'd discovered at the bottom of the pool. As I watched Phil trace his line into the undergrowth, where his back-cast had wrapped itself around a dense blackberry bush, I wondered, not for the first time that morning, what the hell we were doing here.

We get to fish twice, maybe three times a year and in between times we always manage to forget and somehow exaggerate our limited ability until we're as proficient as Zane Grey. And we believe it. The truth is, we could not only do with more river exposure, but probably a few decent lessons and some serious practice. Perhaps we would have been wiser going to a river with better access — something with wide sweeping banks and fewer snags, but according to the report this was the place to be. And more than anything, we wanted fish.

But after two and a half hours in the freezing cold we hadn't caught a damn thing. We hadn't even seen a fish. Trout reports are misleading things. When you think about it, the river that is fishing well, is actually the river that was fishing well yesterday. After that, it's just yesterday's river swelled with today's fishermen. Whatever happens, wherever you go, you'll always find someone who tells you the fish are somewhere else. Not in the lower reaches, the upper reaches. Not the lake's southern rivers, the northern rivers. Well, according to the report we were in the right place — generally. All we needed was some luck.

I looked down at the confusion in my beloved reel — an antique Hardy Brothers I'd picked up at a garage sale for a song — and decided I'd get the better of it sitting down. Phil, already on the bank, was trying to extricate himself from the blackberry now that his line was free, but didn't seem to be having much luck. I waded carefully out of the river, hauled Phil from the thorny clutches of the bush, then sloshed my way to the little clearing where we'd left the gear and emptied my waders. Everything below my right knee was sopping wet. The left was just numb. I wrung out my wet sock, hopping on one leg to keep my foot clean, and put the waders back on in time to join Phil in a contemplative cup of tea.

Although the morning wasn't turning out as we planned, Phil remained unperturbed. So what if we were cold and unsuccessful, losing gear hand-over-fist, we were here weren't we? Isn't this what it's all about, getting away from it all for a day? Grudgingly, I had to agree with him. My feet were thawing slightly, with tea hot from the thermos inside me I'd stopped shivering, and as the sun approached our hidden valley, glistening off frosty trees, I began to appreciate the true beauty of the spot. I looked about, listened to the birds and slowly my enthusiasm began to return.

Phil suggested we try further downstream, closer to the car and I concurred. Both of us had seen the wide stony shores on the other side of the river during our walk up and thought perhaps there, in one of those lengthy, open runs we might find our long-awaited utopia. Somewhere in this river were a lot of fish and we were going to find them. We agreed to cross the river and walk down the other side to try one of these places and while Phil packed the gear I unpicked my reel and broke down the rods so they'd be easier to carry. By the time we set off I was thinking less about the dry socks in the car and more about the fishing we'd come for.

We forded the river without too much difficulty and began, what we thought would be, a brief walk downstream. It was to be our undoing. On this side of the river the track was hardly used. At times it disappeared into the tangle of bush, forcing us to bash our way through wet branches and dew soaked fronds before it reappeared, rutted and narrow. We were drenched in minutes, but we pressed on, neither of us willing to let a bit of bush come between us and our fish. All the same, it was heavy going. Pretty soon it became obvious our early-morning eagerness had taken us far higher up the river than we'd first thought. We remained determined, but as the temperature rose and fishing time slipped away, so did the tension.

We'd been walking for about ten minutes when dodging a branch, I completely failed to notice Phil skirt the edge of a frozen puddle ahead. My foot landed squarely in the middle, crunched through the ice, and sunk into a quagmire that swallowed my leg to mid-thigh. With difficulty Phil hauled me out, but I covered us both with mud in the process, irritating him further. As soon as I'd found solid ground, he stomped off without a word, anxious not to waste any more of our precious time.

In hindsight we must have looked completely ridiculous. Two grown men, childishly petulant, chasing fish by crashing through dense bush in mud-splattered waders and sodden jumpers. With rods in hand, favourite fishing hats glued to our heads and multi-pocket jackets over-flowing with under-utilised gear we were the ultimate in fishing ineptitude — and about as much threat to the trout as a weta in a wheelchair. But hindsight means nothing, we were a long way from laughing at ourselves. Cooking in neoprene and rubber under the mid-morning sun, tired and frustrated, I called a halt.

I took off my jacket, and for only the second time since we started on this poor excuse of a trail I saw Phil's face — and it wasn't happy. Sweat dripped from his forehead, a couple of nasty scratches marred one cheek and a spot of mud had pressed between his eyelid and eyebrow like a Rorschach inkblot. He looked at me and I looked at him. It was somebody's fault we weren't fishing and neither was giving an inch.

It was Phil who broke the silence, wondering, *wondering* if I could tell him what we were doing this high up the river in the first place. Before the words came out I knew I wanted to let it pass, but couldn't. His holier-than-thou tone was just too much. This wasn't my fault, I told him. The trip down this side was his idea, I reminded. As far as I was concerned, it was up to him to get us out and he knew it. Naturally he countered, but I had the old — "if we'd stayed where we were we'd still be fishing" in reserve.

Of course, we were equally guilty and equally innocent. Pretty soon we ran out of argument and stood about glaring into different distances as if waiting for the river to come to us, both knowing how futile our fight had been. Finally Phil said, "Ya ready?" and I said "Yeah" and off we went again.

Not long after that the trail took a sudden dive into the bush and led us up a steep hill, finally emerging on top of a high cliff that protected the river. Our reward was torturous views of the clear, open expanses of water we were searching for, but were now impossible to reach. With little choice we continued, looking for a place to fish as the trail descended the hill and followed the river, deep fast water on one side, steep bank covered in thick impenetrable bush on the other.

By now, as Phil pointed out, we couldn't be more than five or ten minutes from the car, but both of us knew that even when we got there crossing the river would be impossible. And it could be ages before we found another rapid we could ford.

I'd like to think that apart from the fact that there was nowhere else to go but back, the thing that kept us moving was the absence of other fishermen and our desire. Up here we were all alone. Just us and the non-existent fish. So when Phil stopped me to point out the deer tracks he'd spotted, the mud, the sweat, the frustrated fight and the tired heavy legs almost disappeared. We looked at each other and Phil's eyes, those of the eternal bloody optimist, said it again. This was what it was all about. Getting away from it all. It was almost enough.

I still don't know which saw the other first. All I remember is coming around the corner and walking into Phil who'd stopped dead in front of me. The wild boar was obviously as surprised as we were and it did the only thing it knew to do. I'd already turned when Phil's cry of "RUN" ripped the air. We didn't stand a chance in waders and we knew it. I pelted around the first corner as if it were some sort of exotic gumboot race, Phil on my shoulder, but what followed has become a blur. Phil says he was following me and I say he pushed me because the boar was at his heels. Whatever happened, there was track and then there wasn't and I was in the air, the swirling dark blue of the river under my feet one second and over my head the next, the icy cold driving the air from my lungs. I dropped my rod and fishing jacket and managed to break the surface for a breath before the old rubber waders and the current dragged me under again and I felt the bottom. Phil, in his new neoprene's was having a better time of it and if it wasn't for him I'm sure I would have drowned. On the next swirl that bought me near the surface, Phil managed to hook his hand around my collar and somehow between us I got another breath. We can't have been in the water that long before the current swept us downstream and close enough to a shoal on the opposite bank for Phil to get some footing and me to stay above water.

There's no doubt we were very lucky. If the current hadn't pushed us that wide neither of us would have made it. We dragged ourselves out of the river on our hands and knees, both sets of waders full of water. I flipped off my shoulder straps and crawled out of mine while they were still partly in the river, but Phil made it to the shore proper. Amazingly he still had his rod, clutched tightly in his fist like a kid with candy floss. Both of us collapsed on our backs, frozen and drenched and just lay there panting. I'm not sure if I said it, but I know I thought it: so much for deer tracks, *mate*.

Sodden, we left the waders and rod at the river and with no alternative, clambered through the bush in our socks to find the track we'd first taken that morning and hopefully the car. It didn't take us long thank God. We'd already walked most of the way back and the river had done the rest. For a frantic moment I realised the car keys had been in my pocket and as I slapped at my pants, the dunking and all those miles of bush flashed through my mind. Miraculously they were still there.

Without speaking we dried ourselves off and changed into the spare clothes we'd bought in case we'd got caught in the rain. I just wanted to go home. I'd lost my rod, my beloved Hardy Brothers reel, my tackle bag and my best fishing jacket. I was cold and tired and we'd hardly done any fishing and what we had done was dreadful. If Phil had said anything about getting away from it all I would have punched him, but I think he was feeling the same.

We sat miserably in the car with the engine running and the heater on full, still not saying much. There wasn't much to say. We knew that we were the most pathetic fishermen on the planet, perhaps the worst in the history of fishing. But worse, we knew that we still had to face our partners at home. They'd want to know everything. When Phil turned and said, "At least we're alive," I knew this was the only way we could save our egos.

In time the car's heater took the edge off our misery and we shared a bag of potato crisps. At least it wasn't raining. Phil volunteered to retrieve the waders and his rod, but we both went, thinking maybe we could have a look for some of the gear we'd lost. I watched him disappear into the bush, took a final drag on my cigarette and reluctantly dived in after him.

Phil made it to the little beach first and his shout had me turned and moving back up the hill thinking it was the boar again before I realised he was calling me. My hopes rose momentarily, but I knew in my heart of hearts, even if he had found the gear it would be the jacket he found, not the Hardy that would have sunk like a stone taking the rod with it.

But, when I made it to the rivers edge it was better than I could have wished for. Right before my eyes, there on the river's bottom, was the run the radio had reported. There were trout everywhere. Swimming, gliding, fanned out across the river floor. More trout than I had ever seen in my life. More than I thought were possible. Trout with our names on them.

It was the fastest assembly of a rod I've ever seen. Any fool could have taken fish that day, but only a fool smart enough to be higher up the river than anyone else. We took fish with an ease that belied our skill, Phil actually catching and releasing the same fish twice. At times the fish were so eager they would strike at the indicator and not the nymph, and we'd be thrown into confusion.

Alternating the rod and bickering happily over which to keep and which to return, we filled our limit bags without even getting our feet wet. The biggest fish of course, was one that got away, turning tail and racing downstream in a way that made us think we'd foul hooked it. At one stage I even returned to the car for the camera, but the photos of the trout-filled river didn't do it justice. In the end it took us less than an hour to catch more fish than we'd caught all last year. The best photograph is the one taken with a timer, of Phil and I, one rod between us and the fish arranged in front of us. Never have the smiles been so big.

By the time I dropped Phil home it was dark. He stood leaning on the car, peering in my open window, the city lights burning behind him like stars. At his feet was the bag containing the fish. He picked it up, testing its weight.

"Not a bad day's haul, really," he said.

I smiled. "Na, not bad at all."

He looked up into the clear night sky, exhaling heavily as if checking the cold. His breath condensed thickly and he watched as it drifted away, slowly dissipating. In the distance I could hear the sound of cars on the motorway. It had been a long day.

When he turned he slapped the roof of the car sharply. "All right, mate. See ya later," he said.

"Yeah, later on in the week or something, eh?"

"Sure, give us a call," and he paused, shifting the bag from hand to hand. He wasn't moving. "Shame about your reel and stuff, mate," He added quickly.

"S'nothing. I shouldn't have had us there in the first place," I said.

"Hey, next time . . . what d'ya reckon we stay in one place, eh? Let the fish come to us for a change."

"You're on." I said.

"And go somewhere we know."

"Sounds good to me."

"You know," he said, "it's a real pity we don't do this more, eh. We could probably live on trout with a bit of luck."

"Probably," I said, "but you've got to give the fish a chance."

He laughed and slung the bag over his shoulder. "Next time, eh."

"Yeah, next time," I said and slipped the car into gear. "Next time it'll be different."

The Perfect C

Sandra wasn't to know. She believes in 'win-some, lose-some', a percentage concept that I too should trust, but am unable. Unable, because it's not about that, it's about family, and that's the problem.

My father is a winner. When he fills out a form, that's what he should put under 'occupation': winner. The poor bugger. He had his big Remuera house by the time he was thirty and by forty had grown out of the Porsche. He's been a member of every exclusive city club at one time or another and resigned at least once. His business got over the '87 crash the way Germany got over the war, and somewhere in there he even had an affair with his secretary (a lithe, intelligent young woman who was, by all family therapy accounts, a great lay, but who was not, he ultimately discovered, a patch on the wife he loved).

Bored with success by fifty, he decided his life needed a challenge and turned to sport. Harbour swims, lake swims, masters' swims became the norm. Then it was the marathon: half, full, ultra. After that, combinations to test his mettle; biathlons, duathlons, triathlons — corporate, tin and iron.

For five years he filled every spare moment with every possible achievement activity, until, as it had started, it ended. A morning's perusal of the events calendar and the realisation there was nothing left to do. He'd challenged himself into a corner.

I feel sorry for the old coot. He is, you could say, a failure at failure. In anyone else's language, a success, but the fact is, we need to fail. It makes our successes worth something. Without failure, triumph has no value. Life without contrast is bland and empty. And this is my father now, consigned to a retirement of self-improvement and salsa classes

— at which he excels.

My mother on the other hand, has no such problem with failure. Far from being a winner, she is one of the world's contestants: one of life's masses making up the numbers so that people like my father can win.

During my brief exposure to this world, I have repeatedly come home to a living room littered with the entry forms of whatever product's competition she was currently entering. We lived with cupboards filled with cleaners by the case and meals preceded, accompanied, and followed by such culinary delights as potato chips, tinned chilli beans or, when sales were slow, mushy peas.

In the course of her career as a competition entrant she has won exactly one weekend break and one lifetime's supply of medicated wipes. On both occasions she was the only contestant. Never has she branched out to the lucrative world of television and considering her debilitating shyness, never will. Instead, she is destined to devote her daily life to entry forms, the creation of clever slogans and eternal expectation — as distraught by her abject lack of success as my father is by his bounty.

I, thankfully, am different, which is no mean feat considering my background. Growing up, my parents, disappointed by my apparent ambivalence to the world, subjected me to every physical, psychological and intellectual evaluation available. Poked and prodded by specialists, priests and one pretentious Kleinian analyst, my childhood was a nightmare of institutionalised abuse. Rorschach, 16PF, Myers-Briggs were the terms of my youth. Only when I turned fifteen and puberty had set in did my parents accept the diagnosis their battery of examinations revealed. Normal. That's what the doctors declared me. Normal. Middle of the road. Mediocre. The perfect C. My parents were aghast, but I was overjoyed. Success and failure terrify me; the unhappiness, the longing for something more. Each offers only misery.

Which is what the specialists failed to discover. That my mediocrity was intentional and has been ever since. It's something I've done quite well, I think.

From the moment I picked up on my parents' travails I have, unconsciously or not, devoted my life to never attempting anything too difficult, avoiding situations that afforded either extreme.

Throughout school I fought to be average. I eschewed study and assiduously avoided sport. I sat in the middle of the room with practised invisibility and did okay. Now I work for a city council, pay taxes in the middle income bracket and my employment evaluations are forever 'satisfactory'. "Good enough" has become my motto. Yet my success at mediocrity is conditional — I could probably do better. Which apparently, is exactly what Sandra first thought of me.

And why shouldn't she? I thought it of her. Pretty, in a plain sort of a way, intelligent without being overly smart, Sandra was, in the range of mates I had imagined myself with, the mean — someone I could possibly marry.

She worked as a secretary in an office across the road, and every morning we shared the same bus, and every afternoon the same one-to-two lunchbreak. It was a suitably unspectacular romance, composed mostly of movies followed by cups of muddy coffee in places where a cappuccino is thought to be a foreign disease. Quickly we capitulated to couplehood for the reasons mediocre couples should; lack of alternatives, no reason not to.

From those early days our relationship remained blissfully static, characterised by a lack of passion and perfectly average sex. Never were we tempestuous, never did we race back to her place, slam the door and tear off each other's clothes. We made love twice a week — at times agreed by negotiation. We played it safe, lived apart, avoided spicy food and were content.

We quarrelled of course, but like everyone else, always made up. Sandra was a little more ambitious than I, but to balance that, she was more mediocre. Where I had to work at it, constantly aware of plummeting to the depths of failure or soaring to the heights of success, she achieved mediocrity with a graceful elegance possessed only by those who are born to it. And even though her desire for something greater from life occasionally riled me, my apathy and perpetual state of comfort at times infuriated her, so averaging out our differences.

My incredible parents were our only hitch. Resigned to my averageness, they had I think, hoped marriage might save me. Either, that I might marry someone who was themselves extraordinary, or who at least carried the promise that our issue might be. Sandra, innately nondescript, met neither requirement.

It was because of this I think, this desire to gain favour, that made her do it. That, on the morning of my twenty-eighth birthday, made her risk everything and jeopardise our very foundation.

All on the day I'd decided to propose.

I had it planned. Dinner and a walk around the duck-pond where, under the reproduction Eros, I would pop the question on bended knee; 'Will you settle for me?' or words to that effect.

She probably knew it was coming, but while we'd talked about it — the lifetime together, the slightly oversized mortgage, the kids and retirement plan — I couldn't be sure. I hoped she'd say 'yes', expected a 'no' and was resigned to a 'maybe'.

That morning, as I lay in bed turning over the details of my plan, Sandra prepared my birthday breakfast. It was a ritualistic routine. First the food; bacon, eggs, a nice cup of tea, and then the presents. Items I'd requested, socks, underwear, the everyday things before the real surprise — a carefully wrapped shirt or paperback perhaps.

After that we'd spend the day together, and later my parents would begrudgingly visit for an evening drink until we departed for our meal. Little did I know that after so much planning, Sandra would attempt to spoil everything.

The second I finished breakfast, Sandra set the tray aside and began. She was so excited, and it was as I expected. First a little parcel of white underwear, the over-looked price sticker still attached, then a bag of navy blue socks.

"Thank you" I kissed her, "they're lovely."

"My pleasure," she replied and beaming, reached for the gift.

My heart tripped. It was smaller than usual, much smaller, and as I stripped the wrapping neither of us spoke. I peeled layer after layer, my hope disappearing with each one until finally it was revealed. An envelope and card. Disappointment flickered and I hesitated.

"Look inside," she prompted.

I did and suddenly, with a simple saccade, the mediocrity I had worked for sagged, halted, collapsed. The situation I had devoted my life to avoiding, happened.

"What are these?" I stammered, even though I knew before she spoke.

"Lotto tickets," she replied, brightly. "For tonight. A paperback book's worth."

Lotto tickets! For a minute I couldn't speak. The callousness of it all. Lotto tickets! Death or glory. Victory or exile. Visions of my parents flooded through my mind. Win and I'd inherit the unhappiness of my father, lose and I'd be just like my mother.

"Why?," I wailed, "why did you do it?" She couldn't answer, too distraught at my reaction.

We quarrelled, we fought. "They're your lucky numbers," she said. "I worked them out myself. Your birthday, my birthday, numerology." I was deaf to reason. We fought more and then she said it, "Everyone wants to win. You're *abnormal*."

Like an upper-cut it came from nowhere, exploding through my brain. *Abnormal*? Me? Abnormal? She left with the tickets, slamming the door.

That was the longest day of my life. I was paralysed with fear; of winning, of losing; of being my parents; and restless with worry. I avoided everything. That evening when the parents came around for the birthday drink and wondered where Sandra was, I had to confess. Their relief was obvious.

The hour arrived and we had no alternative but to watch. Mother in particular, long banned from the game by my father and addicted to holding any kind of ticket, had to see. On the screen, balls tumbled in the air-jet tossed by providence's invisible hand until, one by one, they began to roll. First my mother's birthday, then mine, then my father's. Mother's smile widened with each coloured orb until it stretched across her face as if painted by a child. Out and out they rolled until I was convinced my nightmare had arrived.

The final ball stopped. Life as I knew it ended. Clouds filled my head. Sometime later the doorbell rang. Disconsolate, I answered and discovered Sandra — in tears, waiting. She'd seen the draw. I couldn't understand why she was crying. She should be happy. The numbers were mine, I was the winner. It was everything she wanted.

"I've lost them," she said. "Tore them up, threw them away. You were so angry."

Dams burst. Relief gushed. My parents smiled knowingly, first at each other, then at Sandra — and then we cracked champagne. Mother toasted our success, father our valiant attempt and failure. I proposed to Sandra.

'Maybe,' she said.

Waiting for the Bell

I watch Jamie take a sip of beer, then glance over his shoulder at the big screen in the corner. Boxing — some sort of Greatest Fights program. Sugar Ray Leonard gleaming in the gym, fists and teeth flashing, mugging for the camera. No one in the bar really watching.

I once read somewhere that mens' identification with their sports heroes was homoerotic — possession and wanting, that sort of stuff, but for all my admiration of Ray's speed and beauty and cat-like fluidity, I don't really see it. Then again Duran was always my guy, not Sugar Ray, and maybe that has something to do with it — or maybe not.

Jamie turns briefly to see what I'm looking at. Immediately guilty, I drag my eyes back to the table. It's been three months since I've seen Jamie — and two before that, and probably the same before that. Now, barely one and a half beers into the evening, holes are already appearing in our post-work conversation like unsightly patches of sweat. Both aware of it, we are equally powerless to do anything. Instead we try to mask each lapse with a friendly smile, or busy ourselves sipping the beers with inordinate care. But we know it's not working and me watching tv doesn't help.

It was never like this in the past. At school we were inseparable, closer than the most co-dependent campus couple. So close in fact, that a lot of people who didn't know better thought we were a couple. But college was more than five years ago. In the meantime, life slipped between us while neither of us were looking and split the foundation of what had once held us together, setting us adrift as if we were on separate ice floes.

Sitting here in this very average sports bar, desperately searching for something to say to each other, I feel sad, almost remorseful because of it. I don't want to lose touch with Jamie, I don't want it to be difficult. Instead I want things to be like they were, like I know they could be.

"Want another?" I hear myself ask.

"Sure," he says without hesitation and I motion for the waitress's attention. At university we had a reputation for excess. Like others we were plagued by our pathetic inability to quit for the night and say 'enough'. The moronic invincibility of youth, I guess. And no one could ever believe how someone as slight as Jamie, seemingly half everyone else's size, could consume so much alcohol without having a near-death experience. I'm still amazed we graduated. That we managed to make any grades at all was a minor miracle.

The waitress finally sees me, but it's a minute before she comes over. She struggles somehow, like she's walking against a current that flows away from our table. Her eyes are flat and disinterested, looking everywhere but at us and I can't help wondering whether she's still in high school or not. She looks young enough, but somehow I doubt it because of the emptiness that surrounds her; as if adolescence left her long ago and now there's only adulthood and she's had enough of that too. I give her the order, but before she leaves she clears Jamie's empty glass and places her hand over the ashtray.

"You guys using this?" she asks laconically and I shake my head. She slides it off the table and slips it into the front of her apron. I watch Jamie's eyes follow her departure.

"Not bad," he says.

"Have you ever actually succeeded in picking up a waitress, Jamie?"

"On duty or off?"

"On. Off doesn't count."

"Then, . . . no, but . . ."

". . . I'm still trying." We chorus the answer rote learned in the past and laugh. He's probably as relieved as I am to be back on common ground.

⟨⟩⟩⟩⟨⟨

We're here because Jamie has just split up with his girlfriend. It's a cyclical thing with Jamie. I see him a few times in quick succession while he's single, then not for ages once he's found someone new. It's always the same. One afternoon at work he calls and I know he's starting over again. We go out, have a few beers, get a bit drunk and Jamie will slag her off — whoever she was. Tell me what a bitch she could be and how he hated being made to feel guilty about watching football on television.

Later, depending how drunk we get and how self-pitying he's feeling, he might even cry. Not that I mind. It's not like I haven't cried on his shoulder before. And besides, we're friends — even if we don't hang out in each other's pockets anymore.

That's why, when he called today, I said yes. Even though I haven't heard from him since he failed to return my calls after the last time he split up with someone and we went out drinking. That doesn't matter. Tonight is another one of those friendship nights, and actually, I'm quite pleased he's turned to me. The only thing is, this time he doesn't seem too concerned about it.

We've been analysing the situation throughout the third beer and for a change, he's remarkably complimentary about her.

"I was upset," he says. "but not anymore. At first I was completely gutted. We decided to end it together, right — our last joint decision. And I was fine for maybe a week. Then suddenly one evening I sat on our bed and cried like a baby, and then, just as suddenly, stopped. Afterwards I thought, 'Right, enough. Get on with it, Jamie. There's gotta be someone to go out with.' And here I am."

"Er... thanks," I say, a bit bemused.

"No, I don't mean it like that," he says quickly. "I mean it's time I caught up with people, you know?"

"Yeah, I know," I say.

Jamie flashes a quick smile and it takes a second before I realise it's sailed over my shoulder and into a different corner of the bar. There's a lot that doesn't change.

"Interesting?" I ask.

"What?... Na, not really," he says.

He picks up his beer and drains it. At the pool table three young guys are trying teach a girl to play.

"I'm going for a Jimmy," he says suddenly. "Get a couple more," and he disappears in the direction of the bathroom.

Just after graduating, Jamie travelled Europe for a few months, spending no more than a couple of weeks in London. It's a distant memory now, but he hangs on to the rhyming slang like he's some man of the world. No one ever knows what he's talking about, but still he persists with it. Anyway ever since then, 'a jimmy' for Jamie, is a Jimmy Riddle — a piddle, and I don't think it's ever occurred to him that it's a variant of his name.

I look about for the waitress again. She's nowhere to be seen so I walk up to the bar aware that I've still got half a beer left. I'd forgotten how fast Jamie drinks. He's almost aggressive, attacking each glass as if personally aggrieved to pick it up and find there's still beer in it. He's on his own tonight. My days of drinking myself into a stupor mid-week are long gone. We don't all have the luxury of sleeping it off in the morning, and besides my ability — not to mention my desire — to deal with a hangover at the office has diminished considerably.

With waitress service hardly anyone is at the bar. Just a couple seated in the middle and an old man alone at the far end. It's like he's claimed the section for himself. In front of him to the right, there's an almost full handle of beer with the empty standing guard just beyond it, and on his left, a cigarette burns unattended in the ashtray. Next to that a racing guide is folded open, a pencil in its spine. He's watching the boxing intently on a small tv behind the bar, occasionally flinching as if ducking a punch. Every time there's a flurry of activity he leans forward and his mouth opens like he's salivating.

On the television Sugar Ray and Duran are in the thick of it, one an armour-plated limo, the other an all-terrain four-wheel drive pick-up; both seemingly indestructible. Duran's hands are low and his brow is furrowed so deep it's almost neanderthal, but he's flicking jabs that catch Sugar Ray like he's standing still and Sugar can't seem to do anything about it.

The bell goes and the old man reaches for his beer and cigarettes like he's been sent to his stool. He takes a long pull at the glass, flicks the round-long length of ash off what's left of the smoke, puffs at it a couple of times and stabs it out, lighting another with a quietly shaking hand. By the time the next round's started he's nailed half the beer and has forgotten about the new cigarette.

I grab Jamie's beer and head back to the table. He's leaning on the wall outside the bathroom deep in conversation with the waitress, so I watch the fight on the big screen while I wait. When Sugar Ray catches Duran with one of those wind up specials, I'm so absorbed in the fight that I let out an audible gasp. The old man looks around and grins at me, like we have something in common. But I know we don't. I'm not a lonely old barfly and never will be. I'm just killing time waiting for my friend to come back. I try to ignore the old guy, but I can't help wondering how he ended up here, old and alone with only his vices for company.

"You hungry?" Jamie asks as he sits down. I notice the old man finally look away.

"What scares you?" I ask.

"What?"

"What scares you?"

"Dying," he says.

"Dying? You?"

"Well not so much dying," he says, "as meeting God . . . Meeting God and finding out that in the life before this one I was a highly devout Hindu only one life away from salvation and now I've blown it. Hearing that I've spent an entire life denying everything my previously highly advanced soul was trying to tell me and now I'm being sent back to the starting line again. That scares me. That and having to remember to leave the toilet seat down. What about you?"

"Prince Albert piercings," I venture and he laughs.

⋖≋⋗

Jamie takes the last chicken wing from the plastic basket, dips it in Ranch and sucks the meat off the bones. He's three beers and a bathroom break ahead and is on the wrong side of drunk. I'm beginning to wonder if it isn't time to go.

For the last hour, since his conversation with the waitress, Jamie's been restless. His eyes have betrayed his lack of presence, wandering over the bar, across the waitress station, marking her movements. In the meantime we've managed to cover school and our last two failed relationships, low input conversations, and now we're on to Jamie's career — which is sort of like being on auto-pilot for him. That is, he spouts his bio at me and I have to listen. It's the kind of conversation he rolls out at networking parties so that he can talk to one person and at the same time look to see who he should be talking to next.

I always forget just how much Jamie is his own favourite subject. But he's got to be I guess. It just annoys me that this is the best we can do.

He licks his fingers, rubs his hands in a napkin, then finishes off by wiping them across his jeans. Ever since he spoke to her, the service has been impeccable and now, as she swoops to remove the basket, Jamie times his delivery to perfection.

"So after all those auditions, I'm right on the cusp, you know? Right on the edge of a major breakthrough," he says to me.

"You're an actor?" she interjects.

"Sure," says Jamie.

"So am I," she says. "Been in anything I might know?"

"You know that vacuum cleaner commercial? The one where the bath robe gets . . ."

"That's you in the robe? Cool."

I know for a fact that while Jamie did the commercial some time ago, he's more recently been doing minor theatre somewhere downtown. Obviously he has priorities.

The waitress stands about awkwardly for a second as if waiting to be asked what she's done, but Jamie's not forthcoming. "You guys want a couple more beers?" she asks instead.

"Not for me."

"Sure," says Jamie and reaches for his wallet for the first time in the evening, but she waves him away.

"On the house," she says smiling. "Not too many stars around here."

"Thanks," says Jamie.

"Don't mention it," says the waitress.

"You know," says Jamie, after she's gone. "As you get older you realise that the value of a good tight arse is wasted on the young."

I slide off my chair. "I'm going for a Jamie," I say.

"A Jimmy," he says.

"Oh yeah," I say.

⋐≡⟩∞⟨≡⋑

Maybe it's because he's an actor that crying comes easy to him. Or maybe he's just closer to his emotions than me. Whatever it is, when I get back from the bathroom the waitress is half-sitting on one of the stools at the table, looking concerned. Her hand is on his shoulder while Jamie's hands cover his face. I know he's telling her about the break-up, and that underneath there are stage tears in his eyes.

God, he's resilient. He's been through more relationships than anyone I know, but he always bounces back. Personally, I think he jumps before he's pushed. He's not the easiest person to live with. We shared a room in college for a semester, but by the end were ready to kill each other. Back then he was messy, dirty and inconsiderate. The archetypal, selfish roommate. As he reports it, *we* did *agree* that he move out, but only after I'd dragged his overflowing and quietly rotting laundry basket — containing half my clothes — out of the room and left it under a running shower.

How easily we forget.

Instead of going to the table I detour toward a beer. I look up at the boxing, then along the length of the bar. The old guy winks at me, makes that clicking noise.

"You're buddy's doing all right," he says, his voice hoarse, scraping out the words.

"Yeah," I say.

"I pulled a few in my time."

"I bet. This still the same fight?"

52

"Na," he says. "The rematch. Waste o' time."

I stand next to him, watch the screen and this time Sugar Ray's got his hands down, sticking his chin out, talking, smiling, doing everything but what they're there for and Duran's getting wild.

When I finally look back at the table, Jamie's hands are off his face and she's laughing at something he's said. I go back and the waitress stands up.

"Hey, I would have got you that," she says, gesturing at my beer.

"No problem," I say with a smile.

She's standing next to Jamie and he's got his hand resting gently on her hip, his arm not quite around her waist.

"I was just saying to Jamie. I usually go dancing after work — at this club just around the corner — and I was thinking, why don't you guys come? It'd be fun."

There's a pause as Jamie and I glance at each other. We both know the score. There's no way I'm going with them, but it's up to me to say.

"That'd be great," says Jamie. "I'd love to. Unfortunately my friend's gotta go. Got to work in the morning, don'tcha pal?"

On the screen Duran's still trying, taking a stance, stepping in, but it's like they're in separate fights. I look at the waitress and nod my confirmation at her.

"That's too bad," she says. "Maybe another time."

"Yeah, maybe another time."

The waitress slinks off, Jamie's hand sliding off her hip as she leaves. He picks up his beer, opening his hand too wide and takes it in an S to his mouth. From over the top of the glass he winks at me.

"You understand, right? This might finally be it," he grins.

Over his shoulder Duran is throwing his arms down in disgust. He's turning his back and for an instant neither Sugar Ray nor the ref are sure what to do. The words, some of the most famous in boxing, are coming out of his mouth as he walks away. *No mas, No mas...* he says, no more, and at that instant I know exactly what he means.

"You're right," I say smiling, slipping off the stool, gathering my jacket. "This might finally be it."

Chana says . . .

Nowadays, whenever I cross the Newton Road flyover and watch the North-western motorway roar beneath me, I am overcome with a desire to play Poohsticks.

This might seem ridiculous, and often does to me later, but here I am again, standing on the bridge fighting that same overwhelming urge. I want to let go of something, watch it land on that obvious river metaphor, then rush across to the other side of the bridge to see it appear again.

Yes, I do find this is a little disturbing.

What I find more disturbing however, is that the thing stopping me is not the possible carnage that might ensue, but the annoying probability that I won't make it across to the other side in time to see my stick or whatever reappear. Not really much point playing Poohsticks if you don't get to see your stick again.

I told Chana about this urge as we were walking back from a café one day. She'd laughed until she'd realised I was serious. "Poohsticks is a game I never got to play as a kid," I explained. "Oh," she said. "You must have had a very deprived childhood." "Not really," I said, but she was already walking.

Chana is very busy person, so we don't see as much of each other as we'd like. University takes up most of her time, so much so that often I go to friends' dinner-parties alone, accompanied only by a bottle of wine and her apology. There's always an assignment due or a tutorial to go to. And when we are together, she is often distracted, lost in thought as her research takes precedence over cappuccino, conversation and the other c of intimacy.

I don't mind too much. It would be nice to share as much time as we did in the early days, but as Chana says, some things have to take a back seat.

Chana says my life is not that great, not what it should be. She's been saying for ages that I should do *something* because she's got university, but months later I'm still working at the Frozen Yoghurt counter pushing fat-free to tourists, not a purpose in sight. Chana says I'm not going anywhere but I hadn't really noticed. Chana says everyone must go somewhere.

The only reason I got this job is because I'd once worked at a Ben and Jerry's franchise in the States. You would not believe how big a person's forearm gets just from rolling ice creams.

I am standing alone on the bridge over the motorway watching cars pass beneath me, dreaming of Poohsticks. Chana is at the conference in Hamilton learning about very important things. That's how I know it's not Chana in the car passing below. Because she's not here. And because she doesn't have a racy little convertible. It looks like her though. Even the jacket is like the one I gave Chana for Christmas.

But I can see it's not her.

My friend Erin says walking is therapeutic. That it calms the nerves. So recently I have taken to walking after work. Instead of walking straight home, I walk around for hours, watching the city, letting my mind wander. There's no real point in rushing home now that Chana's moved out.

Chana says she would like a break. Just for a while. She's felt . . . crowded, she says. Not trapped exactly, just not . . . free. She's felt, she says, like it's not really her. Chana wants to find herself again — and so she should. Chana is a very special person who needs her own space. She is strong and independent, funny and unpredictable. Like a wild horse that allows you to come along for the ride, Chana needs to run free. It's because I love Chana that I've encouraged her to go. She won't be long, she says, it's just a breather. I understand, I say, everyone needs a break.

⊲≈⊱

I must admit that I like my job. Frozen Yoghurt customers are very nice people. Everyday, just before closing, I am visited by two young Asian homosexuals. They are impossibly feminine, too beautiful, and are always holding onto each other shyly, as if terrified of what might happen if they let go. These boys are so in love they might be twins. They take turns at ordering and always have whatever is the special of the day, and I always give them a little extra — even though they're probably rich. They don't talk very much, but they smile a lot. They seem very happy together.

I can't help but wonder if it will last.

Erin comes by to take me to the movies. We leave her car and walk arm in arm over the bridge, down K Rd and into the city. And even though the proximity of her body makes me uncomfortable, I leave my arm around her. I can't understand why Erin suddenly wants to spend so much time with me. She has always been my friend first, but not like this. I hope she doesn't have a crush on me. It's not like I'm available or anything.

Without Chana around, I find I myself walking constantly. And not to the same old haunts either, but to new places. Places that we wouldn't have gone to together. Often my walks take me to the summit of Mt. Eden and sometimes One Tree Hill — although Mt Eden is my favourite. I stand up there, wind-blown and freezing, gazing out over the panorama, imagining what it would be like to leap off into the wind, float there like superman and then land safely back on the summit again. At other times I lie on the grass, stare at the clouds and dream about aliens and spaceships and adventures in distant galaxies. I know that regardless of what I might see, I'd always come back.

And there's a lot to see from the summit of Mt Eden, even on a cloudy day.

Chana will call tonight. She will call and say, "Alex? I'm back". And I'll pause, as if thinking, and then reply nonchalantly, "Okay".

Erin is right about walking and therapy. It does keep me sane. It's where I can let my mind off its leash; let it hare off over distant possibilities, past conversations and future chats; let it race madly over the same old ground exhausting itself. Only when it's tired, can I control it.

But it's not like I haven't walked a lot before. Chana and I walk everywhere together. *Walked* everywhere together. All over the city. The difference is, when I walked with Chana I never saw anything like the things I see now. I would look, but not see, missing all sorts of people. Like my Asian couple from the yoghurt store. I see them all over town. Or the couple crossing the road ahead of me, dressed entirely in black, most of it vinyl.

It is as if they are impersonating each other. They wear the same sunglasses, their hair is uniformly dyed and ragged, and where I can see skin, it is uniformly white. Even their bodies are the same, hipless and lanky; limbs dangling off slender shoulders. But where he is thin to the point of asexuality, she is almost violently sexual, striding booted across the road, daring the traffic to assault her. Was theirs a case of like-attracts-like, or did they grow to this, shopping and dyeing together?

Chana is a firm believer in evolution. Everything changes she maintains. Nothing is forever. Except change, I say, but she doesn't see it. She just tells me to *stop being perverse!*

Chana didn't call, but luckily I ran into her as she left the hairdressers. She was in there for over an hour, having her hair cut into something entirely unfamiliar to me. If I hadn't seen her going in, I wouldn't have known to wait.

She said, looking over her shoulder, that she'll see me later. I've always had trouble matching Chana's stride, but now it seems furious. Perhaps I have slowed somewhat. I don't agree with her. I'm not depressed. Maybe in a bit of a rut, but depressed? Rubbish.

Chana is often saying things about me that aren't true. I am leaving her alone. I just wanted to know why she hadn't called. The problem is, she thinks she knows me too well.

Dougie and I sit in a K Rd café plagued by sparrows. Dougie is Erin's boyfriend, partner, lover, all of the above. Erin is busy today apparently. They're like a tag-team.

We sit and talk, but I am distracted. At another table a couple hold hands. Of everything there is to see in my wanderings, the radical skateboarders, crazy people off medication, street-side proselytisers and other mundane things, this is what I see most, far more than anything else; couples. Everywhere. I never realised how many couples there are around. It's amazing. As a result, I'm becoming a couple expert — and this couple across the room are doomed.

They are anchored to the table by mutual consent, but her eyes drift; over me, Dougie, the other tables, the birds. I know that the eyes always go before the feet, but the feet always follow. I've seen it before. And it's only now I remember Chana's ever increasing extra-ocular exercise. I ask Dougie if we can leave and I walk home.

There's a couple fighting at a bus stop and, when I get home, another reading the news on television.

I have noticed my mind is running less, as if it has realised the futility of chasing shadows. Perhaps it has begun to understand. Eventually ears are made to listen, not simply hear, and eyes must see, not look. No wonder I like walking. Everything is reduced to its barest essentials, the obvious is made apparent.

Chana likes to keep moving, likes to keep going forward at a steady pace. So, what does she see when she walks about the city — apart from the future? Probably little. But for a long time I thought that was the way it was done. That moving ahead, covering distance was the goal. That was until I'd begun stopping and pausing. All the things I haven't noticed!

Where was I looking?

Chana says we should fix our eyes on a goal and never waver. We should strive toward it, focused and determined. She's probably right. Probably.

At the Frozen Yoghurt counter it has become easy for me to pick the lonely people. They are the ones excessively indecisive about flavour, the ones who keep talking for a long time after paying. They talk and talk and talk, not even to me particularly, more at me. The words fill their emptiness. But loose talk to strangers is like beer for dinner — mildly euphoric at first, but ultimately unsatisfying.

When Chana and I walked there were no lonely people on the streets. Now they're everywhere. In doorways, alleyways, suits and ties. They ooze from places I never suspected existed. It is as if I have swallowed a drug that has increased my perception. As if I have woken from a deep slumber. Plainly visible to me is the emptiness throughout this city; the gaping chasms of nothingness that consume thousands; the spaces that no great edifice, tower, or frantic hurly-burly will ever fill.

Instead the city is filled with couples and people alone. There is nothing in between. I should know. When I walk its streets, serve its populace, this is what I see. Everywhere I look there are people holding hands, leaning on each other, day-dreaming at café tables, slumped in urine-sodden doorways, sitting on park benches with their lunches or waiting in the windows of bars for the transformation to occur.

But the city's emptiness is not so easily divided. If the cure was only couplehood, no one would be lonely.

Chana, Chana, Chana. What a name. It sounds like China, Grandma's gaily painted porcelain that breaks when dropped. There is nothing solid about Chana. It's a name without depth. Chana . . . an outline of a name. A hollow name.

⬦——⬦

Erin has my arm again, but when I see the flute player on Queen St I have to retrieve it. Something about his eyes makes me want to stand without being supported. Erin stops easily and we watch him play. Chana never stopped, never went back. He's better than I imagined him to be and even though I have walked past him more times than I know, I don't think I've heard his flute until now.

He stands alone, plays alone and never draws a crowd. It is as if he is playing for himself only. People still leave him something though — even if they don't stop.

We walk on and his tune stays with me.

Chana has written. The letter was waiting when I arrived home. The only letter. I placed it on the table and went for a walk. It's still there. Perhaps I'll have dinner first.

Chana, unwilling to hear my voice, says that I should stop following her — even though I'm not. She says that she's not coming back. That she's met someone else. That there isn't any us anymore and why can't I just accept that and just understand and just get-it-through-my-thick-head-that-it's-over. Why can't I just let go?

I thought I had. I thought that was the point. I let go, you come back.

It wasn't the point.

Chana is a bitch. Not strong and independent, stubborn and selfish. Not funny and unpredictable, flighty and dishonest.

Poohsticks from a bridge over the motorway would be a very unsatisfactory sort of a game anyway.

⬦——⬦

The only surprise is that I am not surprised. I'm not blind and haven't been for sometime. I could sit around the house for days on end or spend time in mourning, but neither of those things appeals. Instead relief cleanses me, takes the heaviness from my stride. I won't have to make up, tie myself down or blinker my vision again.

Like every other day now, I walk past the letter box and keep going. The streets are alive. My walk is weightless. K Rd queens are royalty and the drunken sway of crawling students, a graceful dance.

The sun is in my eyes. I don't see her until it's too late.

Chana blocks my path, says hi, how are you?, it's been a while, and I stop and stare. She says she's pleased to see me. I feel the past build behind me like a wave, threaten to swamp me. Listen... she says.

I look at her, shake my head and start walking.

Cool

"D'you ever have that fantasy of driving across the centre-line directly into the path of an oncoming truck?" asks Chad, examining his sandwich.

Breakfast in Las Vegas. Sean, hung-over, nausea enraged by the smell of rancid fat wafting across the restaurant courtyard, watches blood drip from the meat in Chad's steak sandwich and raises a puzzled eyebrow. It's Sean's first time in Vegas and he's struggling to get his head around it. Chad, on the other hand, seems impervious to the effects of the alcohol. His brown eyes are bright as he talks eagerly through mouthfuls, short hair neat as if he's actually had a shower.

"You know the one. Where you're driving along and death is just a quick twist of the wheel away. You've been watching trucks thundering past you: felt the car rock each time it hits that wall of air they push, seen the trucks' wheels flash past just feet from your window, as high as the car, and somehow you start thinking, 'What if....?'

"Then, when you spot the mother of all trucks barrelling down the road, getting bigger and bigger until it's right on top of you, you can't get the thought out of your head. Your hands don't move the wheel but your imagination does, wrenching it sideways, following the line you'd take under its wheels. In the instant the truck passes, the feeling of the impact — the abrupt halt, the truck coming through the car and crushing you in your tiny tin compartment — is almost palpable, enough to leave your guts sinking and the realisation shivering down your spine: complete power over your own existence. D'you ever do that?" A dribble of sauce escapes his mouth and he wipes it away backhanded.

Sean smiles and shakes his head gingerly.

"What are you looking at me like that for?" says Chad. "It's a serious question. You must have had that thought before." But all Sean's thinking about is what Justine's going to say when they get there and why he agreed to go chasing off across the country in the first place.

"No, I haven't," he says.

Chad takes a slurp of breakfast beer leaving greasy fingerprints on the bottle, then uses the last of the sandwich to mop up some of the juice left on his plate. As the napkin rolls between his fingers and falls to the table, he looks across at Sean's barely touched sandwich. "You don't like it?"

"Not in the mood," he says.

"Want something else, maybe. An omelette or something?"

"Think I'll pass. Stick with the coffee."

"You know, if you eat something, you'll feel a lot better."

"Maybe later," says Sean.

Chad nods, looks at the sandwich again. "Then you don't mind if I. . . ."

"Be my guest," says Sean and he watches as Chad stretches across the table and transfers the sodden mass of bread and meat onto his plate to begin again. When he's finished he leans backwards in the sun, yawns and releases a satisfied, pungent belch that flips Sean's stomach. "Let's get going then," he says.

"I'll drive, eh," says Sean.

Chad pays the bill and as they walk to the car, Sean wonders if it's going to be like this for the rest of the trip, driving all day, drinking all night. He hopes it won't be, but suspects that's exactly what Angel thinks they're doing.

When he'd told her the plan, Angel had set her lithe shoulders and flicked pointedly through tv channels, suddenly amnesiac about the location of clothing he needed for the trip.

"Why are *you* going? she asked finally. "And why does it have to be right now?"

"Because he asked me. It just not the kind of thing you want to do alone."

"And what about me?" she demanded.

"You're all right. I'll be back in a couple of days. Four at the most."

"You just say you're going, and that's it, you're gone."

"It'll be good for us."

"For you, you mean," she said, and Sean felt the familiar surge of irritation rise again.

Neither spoke as he packed, but when it came time to leave it was she who relented, holding him by the door, arching her body softly against his. "Drive safe, Kiwi," she whispered. "Fly home fast" and he'd wondered if they had time to make love before Chad arrived.

Until he met Angel, he'd never been with anyone so beautiful. From the moment he saw her in the university library he was besotted, convinced he could never have her. Yet it transpired that ruggedness, not to mention his accent, had been as novel and alluring to her, as her distinctly Californian beach-girl look was to him. And while the initial, infatuated glow might have disappeared from their relationship, her body still melted the irritations he occasionally felt, as it did then by the door.

He'd kissed her, cupping her face in his hands, but as they began moving away from the door toward reconciliation, Chad had buzzed, foiling Sean's desire with his uncanny timing. She fell away and they'd stood awkwardly for a second until he hugged her, pecked her lips again, and then was gone, heading East into the night, driving down Chad's hopeful idea.

The plan had been to go straight there, but at Barstow they'd detoured into Vegas because Chad got the idea they should relax and 'bond' a little. It's an Americanism Sean hates because it's so now, so facile, reducing friendship to an epoxy resin mix, but it was Chad's car and Chad's trip so they'd ended up in some off-strip bar at two-thirty in the morning, sucking beers and shooting tequilas like they were ducks on a pond.

Only a few weeks ago Chad had been a person who never lost control, a guy whose doctorate was still the most important thing in his life. But in the last month, after everything had changed, there'd been a lot of sitting in bars looking for answers and Chad had caught on fast.

It took less than an hour in that Vegas bar for Chad to get rotten drunk and start covering all the old ground over again — something Sean could handle — but when he'd discovered Chad leaning on the wall next to a pay phone trying desperately to hide the tears, he'd had enough. He dragged him out and they spent the remainder of the night at the back of an empty supermarket parking lot, too drunk to bother looking for a room, only waking when the sun turned the car into an oven.

It was Chad who suggested the steak sandwiches, but Sean who got the hangover.

"You sure, you're all right to drive?" asks Chad.

Sean, not concentrating, is standing on wrong side of the car as if he was back in New Zealand. "If I don't, I'll spew," he says.

"Okay," says Chad tossing him the keys. "Just remember, stay right."

"It's cool. I know what side of the road I'm on."

"Sure you *know*, but I'm terrified your instinct's for the other side and we're gonna end up playing chicken because you, in your impaired state, got confused."

"Relax, mate," says Sean climbing into the car that's already thick with their smell; a disaster of cassettes, fast food containers, magazines and maps, "I'm almost sober now."

They drive out of Vegas, stopping briefly at a drive-thru so Sean can line his stomach with a shake, then continue on, over the Hoover Dam, eventually finding old 66. It'll take longer, but it was the one concession Sean was able to extract from Chad for accompanying him halfway across the country. The desert unfolds around them, mesmerising their addled brains, and neither speaks.

Eventually it's an isolated gas station, a rickety shack with two old-fashioned pumps and some ancient guy sitting out front, that gets Sean thinking first of beer commercials, then of bikini-clad models and then of Angel, so that he asks. "Do you know what you're going to say?"

surprising Chad, causing him to reach for the volume on the cassette deck.

"What?" says Chad.

"Have you though about how you're going to ask her?"

"Not really. Thought I'd just turn up and you know, take it from there."

"She still doesn't know you're coming, then."

"No," says Chad.

"You didn't tell her on the phone last night?"

"How'd you know I called her?"

"Because you always do. Drunk, three in morning. It's like you're waiting for an excuse or something."

"I got the machine," says Chad.

"Leave a message?"

"No."

"Good man. It's those drunk and incoherent 'I love yous' that can really fuck up a relationship."

"Anyway, I want it to be a surprise," says Chad.

"She's gonna be surprised all right, mate. That's for sure."

"You going to phone Angel?"

"Na. She'll be right." Sean glances at the clock. Angel would be at lunch by now. Is that a sign he misses her or merely that he knows her routine?

Staring through the windscreen the road stretches in front of him as far as he can see. Here almost a year already and still he can't get over the enormity of the place, so different from home. Driving it just opens it up more.

"Christ this place is big."

"I'm crazy, aren't I?" says Chad. "This is never going to work. We should just call it off. Turn the car around and go home."

Sean isn't sure there's an answer.

"What d'you think, am I crazy?"

"Maybe. But you will be if you don't ever find out," says Sean.

*

For a while Chad sleeps and Sean watches the landscape change around him, marvels at the sheer barrenness of it all. He wonders why this harsh empty scenery should resonate so totally with him. Whether it's the novelty of it or just his still strung-out mind making more of things than it should. He doesn't know whether Chad's crazy, desperate or what. He can't even answer that for himself.

Surrounded by the desert, hearing only the muffled rhythm of the car, he feels alone like the days he spent fishing as a kid. Not loneliness, but a calm that finally frees him to think. The narrow highway disconnecting him from the everyday life that back in LA, continues without him. Classes, exercise, Angel.

He caresses the notion of not going back, of staying out here, but knows even now that it's the feeling he wants rather than the location. This feeling of solidity, of lightness. He's thought about leaving her before, of finishing it and wonders why he can't. Sometimes he thinks he loves her only ninety percent and it's the ten percent that rankles him. That makes him feel duplicitous. The ten percent where temptation and thoughts of imaginary others lie. She is intelligent and she is beautiful, but there is something spreading between them he can't define. Out here, leaving, just not returning seems easy and it occurs to him that perhaps he remains with her, not because of love, but because of beauty. A way to keep it in his life. Sean shakes his head, smiles to himself. Hangovers.

"How do you think she'll react?" asks Chad from his reclined position.

"I thought you were asleep."

"She might go off at me."

"Who knows, mate?" says Sean. "Whatever Justine says isn't nearly as important as what she does."

Chad sits up and levers the seat-back up behind him. "Last time I spoke to her, she told me she still loved me."

"There you go," says Sean, wondering whether she volunteered the information or whether Chad asked.

Chad runs his hands through his hair. "How long before we get there?"

"Why, you getting nervous?"

Chad doesn't answer, but leans forward and pulls a crumpled magazine from the floor to his lap, then ignores it, staring out the passenger window.

Sean turns his head quickly, glancing into the back. "Man, I'm dry. Is there any of that water left?"

"Nope," says Chad.

"We gotta stop then. I'm dying."

"No problem," says Chad.

At a small town not much bigger than its gas station and craft shop, Sean buys some lunch, two big bottles of Coke and a bottle of generic aspirins. Back at the car he finds Chad sitting in the driver's seat, already belted in. It's only been a couple of hours.

"Mind if we swap?" asks Chad. "I thought you'd want your hands free to eat."

Sean shrugs. "Sure," he says, but he hates Chad's driving.

When they get back on 66, Chad clicks the radar detector to high and Sean watches the speedo rise, until at eighty, Chad sets the cruise control. Sean tries not to look at the road ahead, but each time Chad, not concentrating, drifts the car over the centre line, the thumping beat of the line markers under the wheels sends a jolt through his stomach.

After a while he puts the seat down and tries to sleep, but with his eyes closed it's worse as he follows the car's subtle shift left, tensing himself for the machine gun thud and the ensuing drift back. He's in the wrong place. On the wrong side of the car, on the wrong side of the road, on the wrong side of the world, sitting in the seat where at home the steering wheel would be.

Suddenly the car swerves violently and a truck roars past blasting its horn, flashing its shadow over them like a matador's cape. Sean sits up abruptly, surprising Chad as much as himself.

"Miles away," says Chad and Sean sinks down again, heart pounding.

"Yeah, right," he says.

Only when 66 joins back to I40 and Chad slows down to keep pace with the rest of the traffic does he relax a little.

"I think I'm just going to go straight to her place and wait there," says Chad. "It'd be real dumb to turn up at work."

"Yeah, that's a good idea," says Sean, amazed by Chad's preoccupation.

"I don't want to put extra pressure on her, you know. It's like I've just got to spend some time with her when she's not being hassled."

"Sure."

"Yeah.... As soon as we're together it'll be cool."

"You know where you're going from here?" asks Sean, map in hand.

"Sixty-four North at Williams, right?"

"That's the one, straight into the Grand Canyon."

"The abyss. How very symbolic," says Chad.

"Don't even think about it."

"You ever going to marry, Angel?"

"I said not to think about it," says Sean laughing.

"Seriously."

"Who knows? I not sure she's the one."

"I have this theory," says Chad, "that we get into these really cool relationships with these really cool women. They makes us feel all strong and secure. You know, really strong, like we're really something special. Of course, the next thing we're believing it and we start thinking, 'shit, I feel really good — I can do better than this' and that's when we blow it because we use that strength to get away from them and suddenly we're nothing again."

"Are you trying to tell me something, mate?"

Chad smiles. "Na," he says. "It's just like, until Justine was gone, I didn't realise how close we were, that I really did want to get married." He pulls the tape out of the cassette deck. "What do you want listen to now?"

"Whatever," says Sean. Staying with Angel — or anyone really — let alone marrying them, seems such an unlikely prospect. "You know it really stinks in here," he says, sniffing at the car then at his armpits. He winds down his window and sticks his head into the wind. The air is cooler here with that clean, cold air smell. Much more like home than before.

"There's the sign, man," yells Chad. "Tusayan. No turning back now."

Sean pulls his head back into the car, filled with a sudden rush of impending doom. Chad's blind optimism finally getting to him. "You're sure you want to go through with this?"

"Fuck, she can only say, 'no', right."

"That's the bit we're worried about," says Sean.

"Na, once I get in front of her, it'll be fine."

"Chad, she dumped you and moved to the Grand Canyon."

"She didn't dump me, man," says Chad quickly.

"Okay. She took the job, then she called it off."

"Only because I was being cold. She moved because I hadn't asked her. You know that," and for a second Chad's voice threatens to crack.

Sean realises what he's doing, realises optimism is Chad's only choice. "Yeah, I know . . . I'm sorry mate, I didn't mean to . . ." says Sean.

"It's cool," says Chad. "It's not like I don't know it's a long shot."

⟨⟩⟩⟨⟨⟩

Tusayan, as far as Sean can see, is nothing more than a collection of hotels, gas stations, restaurants and tourist businesses strung along the side of the highway, all serving the South Rim entrance of the Grand Canyon. A gateway before the main event. He finds it a little hard to believe that this was a transfer Justine accepted for her career, even though she'd explained to him that it was a major promotion.

"From small job in big city to big job in small town. It's a great opportunity," she said.

When it had come up he'd tried to be impartial, not get involved, but if he was honest, he'd seen it coming for months and had probably vaguely encouraged her. Not that Chad should know that, of course. It was just that he and Justine were mates, and she was ready to move on. She didn't have any choice. Which would explain why driving unannounced up the highway toward her new life made him feel intrusive; intrusive bordering on treacherous. She'd moved for a reason, after all.

He wonders if he shouldn't ask Chad to drop him up at the Canyon while he goes and does his stuff, but that would sort of defeat the purpose of his being here in the first place. He's still deciding what to do when Chad pulls into the parking lot of the hotel where Justine works. "What are you doing?" asks Sean.

"We need to find out if she's working or not."

"Why?"

"Because if we go to her place she might be there," Chad says.

"Isn't that the idea?"

"No. This has got to be perfect. I want to be waiting outside her place with a bunch of flowers when she comes home. Sort of a pleasant surprise rather than an invasion of privacy."

"So how are we going find out?" asks Sean.

"You have to go into the hotel and ask."

"Don't be ridiculous," says Sean. "I can't just ask if the manager's working, then walk away. You might as well make a public announcement."

"Maybe there'll be a sign, Manager on Duty or something," says Chad.

"Maybe she'll be standing at the desk," says Sean.

"Okay. I'll take you around to her place and you have a look in the windows and see if she's there."

"Where is it?"

"Just around the back, separate from the staff quarters," says Chad.

"Yeah, right! I'm not going around the back to get busted for prowling. Look, let's go and get some flowers, then you can knock on her door and I'll wait in a bar or something."

"What if she's not there?" says Chad.

"Then you wait with the flowers until she arrives."

"That could take forever."

"You're the one who wants to surprise her, mate."

They stare at the entrance of the hotel.

"There's got to be a better way to do this," says Chad.

"D'you want to get the flowers and have a think about it?" asks Sean.

"Yeah," says Chad. "That's probably best."

Ten minutes later they're back in the same parking space, Chad with two bunches of gas station flowers on his lap. "Go on mate," says Sean, "just go and do it. It's six o'clock, right. If she's not home by now she will be soon. I'll be in the bar across the street, if she's not there in an hour we'll both go and get her at work."

"Okay. An hour."

"Unless she's there and you start shagging. Then you've got 'til seven-thirty. Or should that be six-thirty for you?"

"Very funny," says Chad reaching for the door handle. "All right, I'm outa here." He puts his chin on his chest and draws a dramatic breath.

"Know what you're going to say?"

"Pretty much."

"Good on ya, mate" says Sean. Chad opens the door and climbs out. "You'll be fine."

He watches Chad walk toward the entrance, turn right along the hotel frontage, then disappear around the corner. Instead of getting out, Sean slides across into the driver's seat and starts the car. He hasn't got it into reverse before Justine walks out of the front entrance, steps to the side of the doors and lights a cigarette. For a second he wants to hit the horn, run up and throw his arms around her, but quickly decides against it. Instead he looks at her, remembers how not long ago the four of them were going to dinner or the movies or scoring dope from Justine's friends in Venice. Now she's a hotel manager in a tourist town and somehow, across the carpark, it's as if years have passed. She still looks the same, puffing from the cigarette in that quick, nervous way that reminds him of a schoolkid scared of being caught, but seems different, perhaps because of the hair, which has been cut short and coloured. A manager's cut, thinks Sean. A new life cut.

He watches her smoke and remembers the walk back from the liquor store, stoned, half-drunk. How she'd kissed him, and the way they fell into each other's mouths. Chad and Angel waiting back at the apartment while they kissed in a doorway.

When the guy emerges from the beaten-up old Pontiac only half a dozen cars away, he's not at all what Sean imagined she might go for. Tall and lanky with long thin hair, still wearing straight black bartender pants and a crumpled white shirt, he looks like a refugee trendy from the mid-seventies punk scene. As he approaches she breaks into a wide smile, looking happier than Sean can remember seeing her. They kiss and embrace, then she takes the boyfriend's hand, and they too disappear around the corner in the direction of her place.

Sean sits with the car running, watching the corner, thinking about breaking up — why someone always has to get hurt, wishing it didn't have to be like that. How Justine probably meant it when she told Chad she still loved him, but understanding how there wouldn't be words to explain why it's not enough anymore. That sometimes it just isn't and there's nothing you can do about it but leave.

He knows there won't be a scene or a fight or anything. That there'll just be Chad, various pieces of Chad and it will be up to Sean to help him hold it together.

When he does emerge, devoid of flowers, cutting across the other side of the car park toward the bar where they arranged to meet, Sean stabs the horn.

Chad's expressionless as he climbs in. "Well," he says. "That's that."

"Who was he?" asks Sean.

"Not me," says Chad, forcing a wry smile.

"Sorry, mate."

"Na, it was a dumb idea. Come on, let's get out of here, find somewhere else to sleep. In Williams maybe."

"Sure," says Sean, relieved Chad doesn't want to hang around. He slips the car into gear and drives them out of the parking lot, away from the Grand Canyon and back toward LA, toward Angel and the thing he knows he's got to do.

"You all right, mate?" he asks.

"Yeah," says Chad. "Cool."

Brilliant

"One swallow doesn't make a summer," said the lawyer modestly. They were at a dinner party and he'd just won his first high-profile case.

"Maybe not," said Marita. "But it can certainly make your night." The lawyer blushed and Richard watched as Marita lit another Marlboro, exhaled, then threw back the last of her glass of wine. They had just finished eating. She had long, unadorned fingers and blue nails. She was, Richard thought, extraordinarily beautiful.

"Yes, very good Marita," said the lawyer. "But, tell me Richard, do you do fashion?

"I have, but not much," he said

"What about celebrities?" asked Marita. "What famous people have you shot?"

Famous people. Richard squirmed. Corporate catalogues, desirable work environments, the magnificence of corporate success and employee of the month, that was about his lot. And even then it wasn't really his. He was just the assistant.

"We did Ivan," he said.

"Who?," said Marita.

"Ivan," said Sunny. "You know, the old orchardist chap from that gardening show." Sunny was the host of the dinner party and these were his friends. Two couples; the lawyer and Marita, Marcus and Anna; and alone Richard, whom Sunny had invited to take the spare chair.

"Ahh, yes, Ivan," said Marita, but Richard could see that even if she did know, she wasn't impressed.

"What about sport?" asked the lawyer.

"A little, running mostly. We covered a marathon for some clients once. They'd entered a team and had a tent or something."

"A marquee," said Sunny.

"We should do that," said Marcus. He was a banker who liked team events. "We should enter a team for that fun run thing. When is it?"

"Yes," said Anna. "Soon, I think."

"I hate running," said Marita.

"Everyone hates it at first," said the lawyer, "but you soon grow to love it."

"Like anal sex you mean?" she said.

Sunny, Richard and Anna burst out laughing and Marita, smiling, took another drag on her cigarette. As the smoke came out Richard watched her lips and wondered what it would be like to kiss them, to put his mouth to hers and taste the lipsticked smoke and garlic of her tongue.

"What about portraits?" asked Sunny, trying to save the conversation. "Perhaps you could do a portrait of the recently famous lawyer on the cusp of his great career."

Richard looked at the lawyer.

"I'm not famous and I don't deserve a portrait," said the lawyer.

"Oh darling, " said Marita. "Just admit it. You're brilliant — everyone says so. You shouldn't try to hide it. Of course you deserve a portrait."

The lawyer lent sideways and kissed her on the lips.

"Thank you, darling," he said, and while the others smiled on, Richard looked away, then down at his empty plate.

Richard met her again one afternoon a couple of weeks later, not completely by accident, in a K Rd bar where Sunny knew she'd just started work. It was an upmarket place of steel and glass hidden behind nondescript doors, and she was standing in front of the bar next to an ashtray looking more like a customer than staff.

"It's a crock," she said as they entered, "two cigarette breaks in a six-hour shift and they still expect us to smile. There must be a union rule against it somewhere." She kissed Sunny hello and thrust her hand at Richard.

"There's no justice," he said.

"Anywhere, ever," she exhaled, stubbing out the cigarette and moving behind the bar.

Sunny reintroduced them and when the manager wasn't looking she slipped them beers and they listened as she spoke uninterrupted, first of the bar job, then of breaking up with the lawyer, and finally of uncharitable university professors who failed to appreciate her position. Richard listened in awe.

According to her she might as well go on the game as work in this place because she was selling drinks with her tits — the guys only bought extra rounds so they could talk to her. And apparently Mr Brilliant Lawyer never came home before nine o'clock so they never went anywhere anyway, and of course by then he was either too tired or too stressed to be any good in the sack so what was the point? Now she's got to work all hours in this dump — falling behind with social retard tutors who are so divorced from reality that they still think a week's extension is a boon from the gods, and only give it in the vain hope that it might one day materialise into that long dreamt-of student blow-job.

By the time they left Richard felt like a rag beaten clean on the rocks of the Ganges. They walked back to Sunny's car bathed in silence and it was only once they were inside and belted-up that Sunny said, "It was supposed to put you off, you know, not make it worse," and Richard failed to answer.

Later that evening, shaking only slightly but with a pounding heart, Richard unfolded the scrap of paper and punched out the scrawled numbers. He was terrible at this sort thing. Leaving a message was the only way he could do it.

"Hello?" she said. "Hellooo.....?"

"Marita! . . . I . . . ahh . . . it's Richard, from this afternoon?... hi." Stupid, stupid, stupid. She already knows you.

"Hey! I just walked in the door."

Richard imagines her: hair down, struggling to get out of her jacket, the phone jammed between ear and shoulder. "Of course," he said, "you were supposed to be working late, weren't you? I forgot."

"Yeah, 'cept it was dead and so was I, so I took the home-early option — even though I'm *completely* broke. God, I'm so pathetic. I swear I wasn't meant to be poor."

". . ."

". . . So, what's up?" she asked.

"Ahh, that photography assignment — d'you still want help?"

"God — desperately! Are you serious?"

"Sure," he said.

"I thought you were just being polite."

"Yeah, well . . ." he said.

"When? Tell me and I'll be there."

As it turned out she couldn't make it for a week, what with work and uni and life in general, so they arranged to meet the following weekend in her favourite Ponsonby Rd café; a place she said, they could spread themselves out.

It was more than he could've hoped for.

⋘∞⋙

"Trust me," said Sunny, "she's not your type." They were in Sunny's apartment drinking afternoon cocktails. They'd been to a movie. "Sure she's fun and beautiful and all that, but she's not your type. Honestly. You need someone more . . ."

"Conservative. Predictable maybe?"

"*Settled*, Richard. Look, she's great, but she's like a kid with a loaded shotgun."

"Then I'll talk it off her."

"Then you'll be stretchered off, you mean."

"She's fantastic Sunny. Intelligent, irreverent, quick-witted."

"She's quick-witted because she hasn't had a thought longer than three seconds in her life and irreverent because she doesn't give a shit about anyone but herself. I love Marita, Richard, but those kind of people aren't meant to be with anyone. Not anyone like you, anyway. They're

77

supposed to be with equally self-obsessed rich guys, get married and divorced, and have BMWs instead of children."

"That's supposed to be a compliment isn't it?"

"Of course it is," said Sunny.

Richard finished his drink and rinsed out his glass. "You haven't got a beer, have you?" he asked.

⬦⬦⬦

It proved to be an extremely long week. Two days after their phone conversation Richard went to the café she'd chosen to check it out, feeling conspicuous about being there alone, but desperate not to be naive. For days he pondered what to wear, then chatised himself for being ridiculous. He even went back to his old photographic handbooks to brush up on his critique, terrified she would use language he didn't understand.

When the day finally arrived he was early of course, and as soon as he saw them realised what a fool he'd been. The other guy was a painter apparently, a man with an eye. Richard, a mere commercial photographer's assistant, couldn't possibly compete. He didn't even have a leather jacket, let alone a pony-tail. They shook hands, and Richard couldn't escape the feeling he'd been thrown into some sort of gladiatorial contest where the table was their ring and Marita, the prize.

Throughout the session the painter lit cigarette after cigarette. Rolled them, licked them, coerced smoke from them with his sensitive lips and drifted it across the table while Richard examined her photographs, trying to be polite if not actually constructive. It was torture. The painter, as if daring Richard to speak the truth, praised even the most disastrous shots, and Richard tried not to contest every word. Finally after an hour of cigarettes and inane pandering they came to the head shot.

"It's an interesting effect," said the painter, pensively. "The obfuscation of knowledge of subject."

"What?" said Marita.

"The use of light to show we can never fully . . ."

"Oh, bullshit," exploded Richard.

"What?" said the painter.

"It's out of focus and it's too dark," he said. "Who's it supposed to be, Marita?"

"Sunny," she said.

"Really?"

Marita gave a guilty smile. "Yeah. Actually, I forgot to use the light meter and I wasn't sure about the lens."

"Oh fuck," laughed Richard, and Marita laughed too.

"He was a bit of a pillock," said Richard when he phoned to apologise that night.

"Yeah, but such an incredible painter — everyone says he's *brilliant*."

"Right."

"It wasn't very fair to bring him, was it? I just thought he might help."

"Don't worry about it," said Richard.

"So you'll still help me?"

"Sure," he said. "When?"

"You're a doll. Let me call you later in the week when things calm down a bit. Is that okay?"

"Sure," he said.

"You don't think he's gay, do you?" she asked.

Four nights later Richard was still waiting for the call. He glanced at the telephone, changed the tv channel, glanced again, then he picked it up and listened to the dial tone. No messages. He hung up. During the commercial break he decided to make himself a cup of tea but while he was in the kitchen thought he heard the phone ringing. When he got there it wasn't. He dialled his message service just in case but there were no messages.

Back down in front of the tv with his cup of tea he wondered what 'obfuscation' meant and tried to stop thinking about Marita.

✦

"Richard if you feel like calling her, call her." Sunny was looking up at from him underneath the bar of the bench-press. Sunny always went first at the gym. He couldn't lift as much weight as Richard, but he had better abs and could do more crunches. It was where they'd first met.

"I can't call and offer to help her again."

"Why not?"

"I just can't," he said.

Two weeks had passed since the café and she hadn't called. For the first couple of days he hadn't worried, but when a week went by he figured something might be up.

"You haven't seen her, then?"

"No," said Sunny, "but she does this. Disappears for a while, then turns up a month later like it was yesterday."

"A month!" After the sixth day, Richard had called the telephone company to check his answer-service was working properly. He couldn't seem to stop picking it up every time he walked past, but because there were never any messages he'd thought it might be broken. It wasn't.

"She's probably off shagging that painter."

"No," said Sunny. "She definitely dumped him. I went to his opening and he was sulking. He wanted to know what he'd done wrong."

"Don't we all," said Richard. At one point he'd had taken to finding errands that necessitated walking down K Rd, but he still hadn't run into her. When he ran out of errands he'd taken a camera along and photographed things that struck him as beautiful so that he'd have an artistic excuse if he met her. All he ended up with rolls and rolls of photographs and a some interesting conversations with hookers. They hadn't seen her either.

"Consider yourself lucky," said Sunny. "It's like getting off with a warning."

"I don't want a warning. I want to kiss her and hold her and laugh with her — then shag her brains out."

Sunny gave him a look, did a set of weights, then stood up. "Pump this, Richard," he said. "It'll take your mind off things."

⋘⋙

Eventually, of course, Richard did ring. He couldn't help himself. Once Sunny had said it was okay, it was only going to be a matter of time. He'd waited as long as he could but it had become unbearable, like someone had attached his stomach to a rack and stretched it. He couldn't even eat.

"Sorry I didn't call," she said. "I've been away. I met this writer. He's brilliant. He's just about to publish his masterpiece."

"Right," said Richard.

"He was drunk and he proposed to me after only ten minutes. No one's ever done that before so I said 'yes'. He took me to the Bay of Islands to work out the details."

"So you're getting married."

"God no! He was so boring. I thought he'd be insightful and sensitive, but half the time he had nothing to say and the other half he was ridiculously intense. I couldn't stand it so I came home."

"I hope you kept the ring," said Richard.

"He didn't believe in them," she said.

"Loser."

"That's what I thought," she said.

"Right . . ." said Richard, pausing wistfully. "So . . . do you fancy a coffee sometime, then?"

⋘⋙

"I can't believe how good it is!" said Richard. "We've been out like three times in the last week. She's great." It was a month later and they were back in the gym. It was about the only place he ever saw Sunny now.

"She tells me you're having an exhibition," said Sunny. He was deeply tanned after a holiday at some island resort. A medicinal sex holiday

81

apparently. Relationship recuperation.

"It's nothing really. I met this gallery owner while I was taking photos on K Rd. He looked at the shots and . . ."

"So are you just hanging out together or what?"

"I don't know," said Richard. "There's definitely something there, you know. We really click. I'm just taking it slow. I don't want to blow it."

"And what's she doing?"

"The same I guess. I mean, we really share. Like some deep stuff."

"And this is Marita we're talking about?"

"Sunny. Come on! There's a lot to her. It's just a side you never saw."

Sunny wiped his face with a towel and ran his fingers through his hair. "Just don't say I didn't warn you," he said.

Richard made his move on Orakei Wharf. Kissed her while she was framed by the city in sunset, but she pushed him away gently, shaking her head.

"I thought you were gay," she said.

"Why?"

"Well for starters, you were with Sunny at that dinner."

"I was alone," he protested.

"Almost as bad."

"I don't have a girlfriend."

"I still thought you and Sunny were . . ."

"Sunny's not gay," said Richard.

"He's never made a pass at me."

"Is that how you tell?"

"Mostly."

"Marita . . ."

"Anyway, I can't. I'm seeing a doctor now. He's got this revolutionary haemorrhoid treatment. He's brilliant."

"Jesus, Marita. Talent isn't sexually transmitted, you know."

"What the fuck is that supposed to mean?"

"Nothing," he said.

"It better not." She turned back to the water and sighed. "I thought we were going to be friends. I didn't think you wanted . . ."

"I thought we were friends," he said.

The Waiheke ferry cruised past and they stood watching in the cool salty wind. Long after it had gone its wake shook the piles of the wharf.

"We should go," she said.

"Can I call you?" he asked.

"I don't think so," she said.

❧⊱❧

"I'm sorry to say it, but I did warn you," said Sunny. "She was completely the wrong person." They were standing in Sunny's kitchen, where Sunny was putting the finishing touches to a tray of finger food for the party. Richard scooped up a chip-full of Sunny's guacamole and shoved it in his mouth. It was delicious.

"Don't pick!" said Sunny.

"What's she doing now?" asked Richard.

"Being in love."

"Again. Who's the budding star?"

"No one of note. Some old high school boyfriend."

"Wouldn't you know it," said Richard.

"Now, now," said Sunny. "Open some wine," and he disappeared into the lounge with the food while Richard looked for the corkscrew.

When he returned Richard poured him a glass. "I didn't know you were gay, Sunny," he said.

"I know," said Sunny.

"What do you mean?"

"Why do you think I invited you to the dinner party and worked out with you so much?"

Richard looked up from his drink, embarrassed. "You mean . . ."

"I'm well over it," said Sunny, "but you should at least know."

"All that time?"

"Some of it," said Sunny.

"I don't know what to say."

"Don't bother, it was my own fault. I should have known better. It's a bit of a habit." He smiled self-consciously. "Come on," he said.

He led Richard into the lounge where the party was happening. The room was full of Sunny's beautiful friends. Successful looking men and exotic women who reminded him of Marita. He was never going to fall for anyone so completely inappropriate ever again.

"God, this music's boring," said the girl next to him. Richard looked down. She had beautiful green eyes and the smile of a nymph. "D'you think anyone would mind if I changed it?"

"Of course not," said Richard.

She was wearing a summer dress and her collar bones were like alpine ridges. Her hair was tawny blond and straight, and there was a small stud in her nose. She was extraordinarily beautiful.

As his stomach dropped everyone in the room vanished.

"Can I get you a drink?" he asked.

Clocked

They jingle when he walks. No, they jangle. Jingle is what women do. He jangles. Around the office, across the lot, down at the panelbeaters. The remarkably reassuring sound of gold on gold. Jangle, jangle, jangle.

He's got one on his wrist and two around his neck. A nice little collection that took years to get. And he'll be honest about it. He'll admit that he got most of them in the early days of Jap imports when there was still a killing to be made. The days before the public knew about wound-back speedos and weary cam belts, back when the Yen was cheap and everyone just wanted more, more, more. The good old days.

He checks his watch again. In half an hour he can shut the gate on a week that's one day short of the record, the record that two months ago sent him racing to the bank for covering finance. The record he never dreamed of seeing.

It's not a big yard, but sometimes in the past they'd turn two or three cars on a good day. Now out on the road the Saturday traffic's thin and there's no one on the lot. Pretty unlikely to see anybody either. He moves over to the filing cabinet, slides open the top drawer and pulls out the Glenfiddich and a glass from the back. It's been a long day and the scotch cascades gratefully into the tumbler. *The scotch, the whole scotch and nothing but the scotch so help me god*, he thinks ritually. He replaces the bottle, slides back the office door and steps outside into the cool air, glass in hand. Early evening and there's not a cloud in the sky.

The bracelet slips from his forearm to his wrist as he puts the lighter back in his pocket. *Len* reads the inscription — in case he forgets his name, he used to joke. Jangle, jangle.

He looks about. Scotch, cigarette, car lot. He used to do this every night once he'd shut the gates and sent the boys home. Lean against the railing and reflect on the day. Back then it was a form of accounting, a way to get a rough idea of the day's profit while spreading the glow with the scotch. Now if he bothers to come out at all it's just to kick-start the glow with the malt and try and make it stick until he's goes to bed. Probably what made his gut spread so much. He gives it a friendly pat. Not bad for forty-seven considering, and Shirl doesn't seem to mind. Another month she reckons. Another month and if it doesn't pick up then he should get out while they're still ahead. She didn't keep her figure this long so he could go out of business just as her clock runs out. But a month's what they agreed three months ago and he didn't do it then.

He takes a sip of the scotch and tries to imagine closing the place one last time. Sliding the gate shut and putting the padlock on a flat quadrangle of worn, stained asphalt, empty and forlorn.

He can't do it. Twenty years of cars keep popping into his vision, orderly rows, price stickers blazing on the windscreens. He shuts his eyes and tries again, this time imagining driving past and seeing somebody else on his place, but the sign still proclaims it. Len Farris Motors LMVD. Previously Loved Cars of Distinction. He shakes his head to see if that'll dislodge the sign, but it's the girl's voice that disturbs him.

"What about this one, babe?"

His eyes snap open and in an instant he's back inside the office standing behind the glass where he knows the glare of the afternoon sun keeps him hidden.

There are two of them. A couple. Young, threading their way through the rows glancing at prices. His stomach tightens. The guy, nineteen maybe, is in the same uniform as last time. Baggy shorts hanging impossibly low off his hips, black t-shirt under an untucked, unbuttoned short-sleeved shirt, smokes in the top pocket. The same black and white canvas shoes. His hair is short and spiky on top, but at the back a long, ragged tail falls behind his ears and rests on his shoulders. Len looks for the girlfriend, a tidy little thing as he recalls, but she's hidden by cars.

With one eye still on them Len moves to the filing cabinet and places the half-full glass of scotch next to the bottle and carefully slides the drawer closed. Then he takes the emergency Listerine from on top of the toilet, gargles briefly and spits into the bowl. The second time the kid came Len managed to narrow him down to a Mazda and a Honda — both boy-racer cars. The Honda finally went a couple of weeks ago and outside the kid hasn't even glanced at the Mazda. If Len knows his stuff, that's the one he wants.

He pulls the brush from its place in the top drawer of his desk and in the mirror pulls it through his shock of grey hair, making sure the middle parting is clean. He gives his moustache a couple of quick strokes, checks his look, then says to the reflection, "You can do it, mate."

The sound of his voice startles him, tinny and somehow desperate in the office. He turns away, tossing the brush back in the drawer and steps quickly out the door.

Normally, with new clients on the lot, he'd stroll right over and deliver his line. *Hi, my name's Len and before you say you're just looking, why don't you tell me what you're looking for.* But these aren't new clients, these are probables, so as soon as his feet hit the asphalt he's moving in the opposite direction pretending he hasn't seen them, wiping a white smudge of polish off one vehicle, straightening a sign on another. The kid's still a dozen cars from the Mazda, next to a Subaru that's about two grand out of his price range.

For a minute or so Len potters, letting himself be seen but gently closing the distance between them. This is the bit he likes, stalking. Circling the kid as the kid circles the car. He's pretty cool, thinks Len, most people would be right next to it by now. But the kid is still busy with the Subaru. It occurs to Len that he might be wrong about the Mazda, that maybe the kid got some bucks from his old man or something and really is into the Subaru. If that's the case he's going to have to rearrange his plan. He thinks about it for a second, then decides to move out into the open and notice the kid, but as he does the girlfriend appears next to the Mazda. He'd forgotten about her.

"Is this the one?" she calls. Her voice is high-pitched and eager. "Is this it, Daz?" Len flicks to the kid whose shoulders fall for a second, then lift as his head nods a nonchalant affirmative.

Gotcha, thinks Len. He turns, and over four roofs (one hatchback, two saloons and a station-wagon) says to the girl, "She's a nice car that, luv . . . but there's a better one over there."

The Mazda is red. Interior, exterior. Every surface visible to the eye excluding the windscreen — and the kid loves it. Which is why Len's got them standing around the Toyota. To increase the desire, create a little desperation; the Toyota the kind of car the kid's mother would drive. Already the kid's started to fidget and more than once he's glanced back at the Mazda, but Len keeps on, sitting him in the driver's seat, showing him the engine.

"Yeah, I wrote out the check for this one myself. It's no trade-in. Actually, the guy I bought it from has been buying cars from me for years. He'd bought it for his daughter, but apparently she wanted to do her big OE, so here it is."

"Right," says the kid

"Nice and straight, never been pranged. Runs like a dream. I had a full service done as soon as I got it here and I'll tell you what mate, inside she's beautiful, clean as a whistle. Exactly what you're after."

"Okay," says the kid, noncommittally. He's standing back as Len talks him around the car, apparently unwilling to get too close. As if engaging with the car, touching its secret places for rust is some sort of infidelity against the car he loves.

"The tyres are practically new. New wiper-blades... What else can I tell you?"

"I dunno. I mean, yeah, it's all right, but . . ."

"But it's not quite right, is it? You're looking for something a bit different."

"Yeah, different."

"What kind of different? Bigger? Faster? What?"

"I dunno . . . not faster exactly . . ."

". . . But *classier*. Something a bit brighter maybe?"

"Yeah," says the kid slowly cracking a smile. "Something a bit brighter."

"Like that Mazda?"

"Yeah," he says. "Maybe."

"Right-o," says Len. "Let's go."

They turn away from the Toyota and the girl slips past to follow her boyfriend, her hand brushing against Len's leg. He'd forgotten how cute she was. Mousey almost. Small and slender, a couple of years younger than the kid, black hair cut into a bob, her long neck disappearing into a baggy sweat-shirt. As they squeeze between the cars single-file, Len's eyes fall to her pants, tight black boot-leg hipsters that cover her cheeks like cling film, not a knicker-line in sight. Her thighs barely touch as she walks. Jesus, he thinks. Not bad, not-bloody-bad. She wasn't that hot last time.

Ahead the kid's already at the car, drifting his fingers along the side-panels as he walks by. It's unconscious of course, but Len notices and his pulse quickens. The kid wants it bad. He moves quickly around to the driver's side and retrieves the keys from behind the sun visor, starting the car with a roar.

"What d'ya reckon?," yells Len, giving the engine some gas, "not bad, eh? You wanna take her for a drive?"

The kid, prowling around the front, pauses, then scrunching up his nose, shakes his head.

Len looks at him puzzled, but the kid doesn't elaborate. Just stands there listening intently to the engine. Len revs it again and the kid frowns, then abruptly drops to the ground and slides underneath the car.

Go for it, thinks Len. Nothing to see under there. He looks across at the girlfriend who's leaning against the car on the left, her head cocked to one-side, arms folded across her chest, legs tapering into expensive-looking running shoes. The fabric across her hips is flat and tight. Christ! He glances over the bonnet for the kid, but there's no sign of him. She must be wearing knickers. Surely. He looks back and she flashes him a smile. Len's stomach stirs and he smiles back. What he could do with that.

Under the car the kid is tapping something. Come on you little shit, what do you think you're going to find? In the office, the weekly sales board remains empty. Len glances around the car's interior, makes certain everything's okay, then drums his fingers against the steering wheel. Catching the girlfriend yawning he looks at his watch jokingly and she laughs, revealing small white teeth. She looks towards the kid, rolls her eyes and makes the 'crazy' sign with her finger at her head. Len lets out a chuckle. He's still smiling when the kid reappears and signals him to pop the lid.

Leaving the car idling Len joins him under the bonnet. "Beautiful," he says. "These rotaries are something else, aren't they."

"Yeah," says the kid. "How many Ks again?"

Christ, thinks Len, if you played your cards any closer to your chest it'd be open heart surgery. "One-twenty," he says pulling out the dipstick, "but you wouldn't know it. Look at that oil. Good enough to drink."

The kid steps back and Len puts the lid down gently. "Two owners, factory new, all mod cons including designer interior." He walks around to the passenger side and opens the door for the girlfriend. "Get in," he says to them both, "feel her out." The kid gets into the driver's seat and the girl climbs in next to him. Len leans down beside her to demonstrate. She smells of sweet, green apples. "That's five hundred bucks worth of stereo right there to start with, plus it's got a light on the mirror here, a/c, cruise control . . . all the bells and whistles."

"I don't know about the colour in here," says the girl. Her hair is inches from his nose. The urge to bury his face in it and breathe is overwhelming. "What d'you think, Daz?" The kid doesn't answer, just shrugs his shoulders.

"If colour's the only thing I'll throw in a couple of seat covers. Colour's easy."

"Really?" she says, excitedly.

"Sure," he says.

He stands up, leaving the two of them in their seats and walks around to the front of the car. Looking at them admiringly he brings his hands to his face, says "Hold it," and quickly snaps a pretend photograph.

"Perfect," he says. "It's you."

The kid pretends not notice. Instead he examines the dashboard then turns on the stereo, flicking through stations until he finds something he likes. When he does Len doesn't know what it is, only that it's not the Eagles. "Turn it up," he says, "give it some volume." The kid does and a wave of pounding bass shudders the car.

"Beautiful," says Len, beaming.

They sit in the front seats, the kid poking around, girlfriend nodding her head to the music while Len watches, happy to let them sell themselves the car. Eventually, apparently satisfied, the kid kills the engine and climbs out. The girlfriend, obviously sick of hanging about, stays seated.

Watching the kid get out, Len knows what's coming. At the kid's age Len was exactly the same. First check everything you possibly can, say nothing, then take it for a drive. As soon as you get back, start tyre-kicking. Stand about and point out everything that's wrong. Once the guy's sweated a bit, you tell him what you're prepared to pay. It's a ritual, and for his part Len's got to hold his ground, pretend his five hundred dollar cushion doesn't exist.

"So what'd ya reckon?" he asks the kid. "You wanna take it for a drive?"

"It's been clocked," says the kid bluntly.

"Eh?" It's like someone's smacked him in the chest. He's never been accused of that before.

"You know, wound back. Done more Ks than . . ."

"I know what clocked is," says Len, every millisecond of experience keeping his voice at something approaching normal. "But not by me, it hasn't."

"Yeah, well I reckon someone has. Most of them have been, y'know."

"Maybe," says Len. "But we changed the cam belt when we did the service and there's no way it had done any more Ks than are on the clock."

"You still got it?" says the kid.

"The cam belt? No, I don't have it!"

"How come? You had this car a long time or something?"

Len looks away, runs a hand through his hair, then forces out a laugh. "Jesus kid," he says gently. "What d'you think?"

"I dunno what to think," says the kid, "but I reckon it's been bogged too."

If Len didn't need to sell the car so badly he'd drop the little shit. Grab him by those half-off-the-arse pants and throw him clear across the other side of the road.

"Listen," he says slowly, fighting the rage in his voice... "Whatever you think . . ."

"Jeez, it's hot in there . . ." It's the girl. "Like an oven." He didn't realise she'd got out of the car, but there she is, pulling off her sweat-shirt.

"That's because it's been in the sun all . . ." says Len, but doesn't finish. Beneath the girl's sweatshirt is a tiny lycra top and in the middle of her bared stomach a silver stud marks her belly button. Close to it is a small tattoo. She smiles coyly, and Len swallows, feels a different heat rising. *Jesus*. Unsure where to look he turns to the kid who's staring at the car.

"I need to piss," says the kid. "You got a toilet?"

"Don't mind, Daz," she says, once the kid's left. "It's just his way. He just says what he thinks."

She's standing inside the open passenger door, one hand on the roof, the other resting on the door frame and Len wants her to walk again. She's got breasts like pop-up headlights and an arse like... like... like a great arse. It doesn't get this good every day of the week.

"Well, what d'*you* think?" he asks.

"It's pretty cool," she says, "but it's not up to me."

"You've got to be seen in it."

"Yeah, maybe." She turns around and takes another look inside. Len can't get over how slender she is. Like a young Shirl. Back in the old days she would've been just his type. Would've had her in the back seat of the Holden quicker than you could say 'big block'.

"You want a cigarette?" he asks.

"No thanks," she says, shaking her head with child-like exaggeration, "can't stand them."

"So," he asks, "you guys been going out long?"

"Oh, yeah," she says affirmatively, " 'bout six months."

"That long, eh," then immediately wonders what to say next. Nothing comes to mind, so he lights up and in silence walks around to the back of the car. "Open the boot will you, luv?" She does and he raises the hatch. "Plenty of room in here, and the seats go down. Does he surf?"

"Na, he's a musician."

"Drums?"

"Guitar and amp. Sorry."

"Just trying to make sure he gets what he wants." She still hasn't left the passenger door.

"He will," she says. "He always gets what he wants."

"I bet," says Len, taking a drag on his cigarette. "What about you? Do you always get what you want?"

The girl smiles. "Probably what I deserve," she says. Len can't tell whether she's flirting or not.

"So, you got a car?"

"Nah. Dad won't let me 'til I'm twenty. It's like such a pain."

"Sure," says Len. Smart Dad though, he thinks. If she was his daughter he wouldn't let her have one either.

He shuts the boot and takes a walk around the car. He knows it inside out, but it's never too late to spot something.

"Hey, do you think this is going to take much longer? I'm s'posed to be home for tea in an hour."

Len looks at her. She's back on the edge of the passenger seat kicking pigeon-toed at an oil-patch on the ground. The sun has fallen behind the offices across the road casting shadows on the lot and there are goosebumps on her arms. He wonders why she doesn't put her sweat-shirt back on but then realises that she's probably not allowed to, and his dislike of the kid moves up a gear. Christ knows what she's doing with him.

"Dunno luv," he says. "It all depends on your boy."

"Great," she says, falling back into the seat, "just great." She looks like she's going to sulk. Shit, he thinks, she's just a kid.

"Look," he says. "Why don't you go into the office and make yourself a cup of tea or something. It's warmer in there and there's some maga—zines and a radio. I'll try and push it along a bit. If he really wants it . . ."

"Nah. Thanks all the same, but Daz'd kill me if I didn't hang about."

Len looks back at the office and sees the kid making his return between the rows. About time, he thinks, but it's dread that fills his stomach. He wonders whether it's worth it, knowing full-well that it is. That it has to be. That another half an hour will see the car gone and the dry spell over. Everything will be all right and Shirl will be happy again.

He walks over to meet him. "Better?"

"Much," says the kid, smiling broadly. "Let's go for a drive."

"Sure," says Len, puzzled by the sudden attack of enthusiasm. "You like it, then?"

"Oh yeah. It's just those Ks that are a bit of a worry. But we can sort that out later, eh?"

"Yeah, probably," he says. "You don't mind the colour?"

"Nah, mate she's sweet. Let's go."

"Righty-o," says Len and they turn to the car, but before he can take a step the kid's got his hand on Len's arm, restraining him as if sharing a secret.

"Look at it," he says, smirking. "Not bad, eh?"

"A classic," says Len, now relieved by the transformation.

"Not the car, mate. *Her*. Don't ya reckon she's hot?" The girl is still waiting for them. "I reckon she'd go off in the back, don't you?"

Len looks at her slumped in the passenger seat, picking at her nails, occasionally rubbing her arms. So small she looks like she'd fold if anyone even yelled at her.

"I reckon she looks cold," he says.

"Yeah, yeah, but think of that arse. Doesn't it make you just wanna give her one?"

Len looks at him. The kid's nose is covered in blackheads and the angry ridge of pimples around his chin seems volcanic. He wonders how many car yards the kid's dragged her to dressed like that as part of this 'piss him off first then make friends with him later' charade, or how much swilling she has to sit through until he's ready to start pawing her. Bloody rev-heads. Screwing up everyone else's lives with their empty, go-nowhere promises; never giving them what they want, what they deserve. Christ, she's young enough to be his daughter.

"No, it doesn't" he says.

"Really, mate?" says the kid walking up to the car and smiling at the girl. "Oh well, one man's meat, eh?"

"Bugger off," says Len.

The girl looks at him uncertainly, then stands and hangs on to the door.

"Eh?" says the kid.

"You heard," he says. "Get off my lot. You too," he says to the girl throwing her the sweatshirt that's been sitting on the roof of the car. "And put some bloody clothes on before you catch a cold."

The kid starts to protest, but Len gets in his face, walks him backwards swearing at him; Clocked! Bogged! Smart-arse little shit... *dragging her around car yards half-dressed, should be ashamed of yourself.* He knows he's being ridiculous, yelling, waving his arms, but he keeps the kid moving, past the wagons, the utes, the vans, the racers, the family and the work cars. Past the flags and the stickers and the great deals, the oil stains and the cracks, until finally they're off. Out the gate. And he can slide it, clanging shut, behind them.

Breathing heavily he makes the long walk back to the office and retrieves his scotch from the drawer. He tops it up, falls into his chair and takes a slug, the empty sales board reflecting his shadow. He's shaking. She could have been his daughter.

Fuck it, he thinks, I'm too old for this crap. Too old and too bloody soft. He picks up the scotch again, swallows, then speaks to the picture on the desk.

"Sorry Shirl," he says.

Panadeine

The headaches began not long after Jeff's girlfriend started cheating on him. She had only leap into bed and within minutes his cortex was a writhing knot that no amount of Panadeine could alleviate. It wasn't difficult to make the connection and it was how he tracked her progress: across Europe, through the Middle East and into the sub-continent.

Europe was the worst, of course. The allure of accents and the novelty of her new found freedom ensured Jeff continued and prolonged discomfort. Mercifully she'd moved on, and there was a repose until Morocco where she'd hooked up with some French guy, mainly she explained in a letter, for security; but nights are cold in the desert and Jeff had found the time-difference particularly inconvenient. Fortunately, by the time she'd made it to India she'd lost Frenchy and had contracted a solid case of Delhi-belly, which, in combination with the heat and the filth and the actual drudgery of travelling, slowed her somewhat, making Jeff's life a little easier.

Not surprisingly, her letters and e-mails mentioned nothing of her affairs, filled instead with euphonious descriptions of 'great times' and 'this neat guy', but Jeff knew. And if on occasion his head didn't tell him, his battered heart would.

Ron thought he was crazy.

"Jesus Jeff," he said, taking a sip of beer, handing the can back to Sally, "it's too much. Next you'll be having nose-bleeds when she orgasms."

"Leave him alone," said Sally. "Anyway, it'd be amazing if he did."

"Can we not talk about this?" asked Jeff. They were supposed to be taking him away for the day.

They were in Ron's car on the way to the beach. Had been for an hour already. Jeff in the back, the still-new couple up front, the odour of dog, sun-cream and sweat-soaked upholstery all around. It was almost working, but every time Jeff nearly shook the heaviness, Ron would open his mouth.

Jeff lowered the window. There hadn't been any loyalty oath between them because it hadn't arisen. They'd just sort of drifted up to the day, then said goodbye at the airport. When Jeff had walked away with Sally and a couple of other friends, he'd just felt cold. Not numb like they say, just cold on the inside and a bit fuzzy, like something important had happened, but he wasn't sure what. It wasn't until the headaches started that he'd worked it out.

And now he was pining for her. Dreadfully.

Ron slowed and turned onto a metal road. Dust immediately filled the car forcing Jeff to imprison himself behind the window again. Thank God they didn't bring the dog.

"So where exactly are we going?" he asked.

"The perfect place for you guys to learn," said Ron.

"I'm still not convinced this is such a great idea," said Jeff.

Sally twisted around from the passenger seat and put her hand on his knee. "Oh come on," she said, "it'll be fun. When did you last try something completely new?"

I'm twenty-seven, thought Jeff. Where does it say I have to keep trying the new? "I just don't like swimming that much," he said. "I'm not that confident in water."

"Surfing ain't swimming, Jeff, it's a state of mind." said Ron. "Trust me on this one. One good wave and you'll be hooked for life."

"Either a wave or a surfie-chick," said Sally. She was trying hard to make it better.

Jeff stared out the window at the flat, brown farmland around them. In the distance a farmer was on a tractor, a tall plume of dust marking his passage. She was only supposed to go for six weeks. That was her original idea. But somehow that got extended to eight, and now it was twelve with no real date of return. He still didn't know if they'd broken up yet.

"Jeff. Yo, Jeff!" Ron was looking at him in the rear-view mirror. "Throw me a beer, man." Suit to surfer in the flick of a tie, thought Jeff. Only in advertising.

He put his hand in the chilly bin, hunting out a can for himself too, testing each with a squeeze. The ice had partially melted and some of the cans, the ones Ron had left in the freezer overnight, were still defrosting. Sally and boyfriends — she could really pick them. He handed a can between the seats.

"Sally?" he asked.

"No thanks," she said. "Might need to drive . . ."

Jeff sat back and returned to the window, cracking it open as Ron lit a cigarette and put on some surfer music. After a time Sally turned around again, smiling softly. They'd been friends since school; Jeff knew what was coming. "You're awfully quiet back there," she said finally.

"Just thinking," he said.

"You'll get a headache," warned Ron.

"Or a nose-bleed," laughed Jeff. Ron hadn't meant it like that, but it worked anyway.

When they arrived, Jeff was the first out of the car. In front of them the beach sprawled away on either side; rolling sand dunes acned with tussock, gently sloping sand and then a sea that was as calm as a sleeping hippy.

"Shit," said Ron from the other side of the car. "Shit, shit, shit."

"We can still swim," said Sally.

"It's not the point," said Ron.

Across the carpark some kids were strapping boards onto roof-racks.

"Hey Matt," called Ron. "What happened to the surf?"

"It was good this morning, man, but the swell swung north. Killed it big time."

"You're outa here?"

"We're going up the coast. To Jack's Bay," said Matt.

"Right," said Ron. He turned to Jeff and Sally. "That's the surf report. What do you guys want to do?"

Sally glanced across the bonnet to Jeff. "I don't know," he said. "We're here now . . ." The idea of getting back in the car was, in the short term at least, repugnant.

"And I wouldn't mind a swim," ventured Sally.

"It's your call," said Ron.

Sally looked over at Jeff again. He shrugged.

"Are you sure that's okay, Ron?" she asked.

"Yeah," said Ron.

They opened the back doors and Sally retrieved her kit, and with difficulty, the chilly bin. "Can you get the umbrella, Jeff?" she asked. It was on the roof next to the surfboard.

"But I thought you just wanted a swim," said Ron. Jeff froze.

Sally looked at Ron. "Yeah . . . and a bit of a read... you know."

"So we're not surfing, then? At all, I mean."

"Well . . ."

But Ron was already jerking at the straps around the umbrella. "It's just that when you said you wanted a swim, I thought that's what you meant, you know, just a swim . . ."

"Is that not okay?" she asked, puzzled.

"It's fine," he said. He slid the umbrella off the rack and handed it to Jeff. It was covered in a garish faded floral pattern and there were spots of mould around the crown.

Jeff laid it down and moving to the back seat slipped into his canvas shoes. Sally was using the sun-block. She proffered it to Ron, but he shook his head, so she passed it to Jeff who smeared the cream liberally over his face and neck while Ron watched piteously.

Jeff handed the cream back to Sally and they assembled themselves next to the car, finally ready: Jeff with umbrella, Ron with the chilly bin on his shoulder, Sally and her bag.

"Right," said Ron, "everybody set?" Sally and Jeff nodded. "Then . . . Onward Christian soldiers," he declared, and they marched onto the sand.

They left it up to Ron to decide which was the best place for them to be, and he stopped not far from the car, but not close; still on the soft sand, but away from the dunes. There was hardly another soul on the beach.

"So tell us more about the headaches," said Ron, once they'd set everything up. He was sitting in the sun on top of his chilly bin, yet another beer in hand, cigarette between his fingers. "It's bizarre."

"Not now, Ron. Leave it alone," said Sally.

"No, I'm interested, really."

"There's not much to tell," said Jeff. "Sometimes you just know."

"That she's cheating on you."

"Yeah."

"Even though she's in Europe or whatever."

"India now. Yeah."

"How long were you going out before she left?"

"About a year."

"But you didn't get headaches immediately?"

"Ron!" said Sally, looking up from her book. "What's up with you?"

"Na," said Jeff.

"I'm just trying to figure it out," he said.

"You're interrogating him."

"No, I'm not, am I, Jeff?"

"A little," said Jeff, shifting again. Sally had sprawled out lengthways under the umbrella and Jeff was having trouble staying in the shade.

"Sorry, mate," said Ron. He dropped the cigarette butt onto the beach and toed some sand on it. A zephyr of silence drifted over them.

Jeff closed his eyes. He heard the sea, Sally turn a page, then the crack and slurp of a new can.

"Bet you've had some great dreams," said Ron eventually.

Sally dropped her book. "Now you're just being a wanker," she said coldly.

"It's a joke!"

"Yeah, well . . . your girlfriend hasn't just fucked off on you to root her way around the world, has she? — sorry, Jeff."

"No, but you won't, will you?" said Ron. "Not with those gems in your ears."

"Oh great! I'd like to think that us being together has a bit more to it than just you buying me things."

"Of course it does, but it's not like they're actually together, is it?"

"Ron!"

"Well, it isn't. She might have done it badly, she might even be a cowardly bitch, but I'm sorry, I'm not convinced she's doing anything wrong."

"He's got a point, Sal," said Jeff.

"Get off the grass," said Sally. "You don't believe that and neither do I. It's not over till someone says so."

"Fine," sighed Jeff. 'It's over'. Someone said so."

Sally smiled at him sympathetically, but he could sense her anger radiating.

There was a slight pause then Ron said, "Have you ever rung her, you know, to find out?"

"Oh, for fuck-sake," said Sally, standing abruptly. "I'm going for a swim."

"But I'm intrigued," needled Ron.

Sally didn't answer, instead turning quickly and running over the hot sand to the sea. Jeff watched her go. He didn't relish the idea of being left alone and defenceless with Ron.

"I guess I'm in the shit," said Ron, joining him in the shade.

"Probably." Sally was already up to her knees, splashing water over her arms and body, a sure sign it was cold. Then again, the sea always looked cold to Jeff. "Why do you bait her like that?" he asked.

"I don't know," said Ron. "Sometimes she bugs me."

Jeff picked up Sally's book hoping Ron might take the hint. He wasn't sure how much more he could take. The book was four hundred pages of solid paperback beach fiction; true love, couples, treachery. He put it down quickly. Behind him Ron was working on his beer.

"So you must really love her, then" said Ron.

"What?"

"You must really love her. Otherwise you wouldn't . . ." but Jeff had turned away and was staring out to sea. At Sally lying on her back kicking up a fountain, at the diving birds, at the blue that went all the way to the horizon. He took a few seconds to answer.

"Yeah," he said quietly, "guess I do." It was the first time he'd admitted it to anyone. He shifted in the sand. It'd be all right if she didn't keep in contact, then he could just forget her.

Something cold touched his shoulder and when he turned he saw it was Ron offering a beer can. Jeff shook his head. "You want a swim?," he said. "I'm going in."

"Na," said Ron. "I hate just swimming."

Jeff slipped off his t-shirt and stepped out of his shoes. "See ya soon," he said.

"Sure," said Ron.

The water was cold, but not nearly as he'd expected. In the distance Sally was swimming bad butterfly, arms flapping on the surface like a wounded gull. "C'mon," she yelled, standing. She was about forty metres off-shore and up to her armpits. "It's really warm." A relative concept, thought Jeff.

He began to wade gingerly waiting for the depth, but once he was waist deep the bottom sloped only slowly away. His admission of love was still with him. He'd managed to avoid it for so long, but now it was out. Damn Ron. It was none of his business.

Ahead, Sally was getting impatient. "Hurry up!" But Jeff waved her down, stopping to acclimatise. It was still colder than he liked.

"C'mon slow-coach," she said. She'd given up waiting and had swum over.

"Leave me alone, I'll be fine."

"Yeah, by low-tide." She reached over and took his hand. "You've just got to get in."

"I've been in," he said. "Last year. It was wet."

She was half-swimming half-walking in front of him, her shoulders still submerged, brown hair plastered to her scalp. She took a mouthful of water and squirted him like a fountain. "Sorry about Ron," she said. "He's acting very weird."

"That'll be the beer."

102

"Normally he's a real sweetie."

"He's worried you're angry at him."

"Not really. Annoyed more than anything." The bottom slipped away abruptly and she had them out to their armpits again. "Sometimes, he can be quite special."

"You mean like, *'I'm special'*," his voice thick like a retarded child.

"Don't mock," she said. "It's awful."

"Well really, 'Bet you've had some good dreams'. What's that all about?"

Sally laughed. "I told you, he's special."

Jeff took a deep breath and sank under the surface. Pushing off the bottom he burst into the air. "Special!" he yelled, waving his arms and crashing back into the sea.

Sally laughed and swam a few strokes away to better splash him, swinging her arm in an arc across the surface. Jeff returned fire, directing a plume of water that landed in front her face and she squealed with delight. Behind her he could see Ron waving. Jeff waved quickly and splashed her again. Ron was approaching, halfway down the beach and still waving. Cell phone, thought Jeff. He was about to speak when he saw what Ron was waving about; there between Sally and the shore; the tip of the dorsal fin and occasionally, twin wavering lines where the tail would be.

Jeff was struck by how slowly it was going, so used to movie ideas of them powering through the water at breakneck speed. He watched it for a second trying to gauge it's length, mesmerised by the lazy sweep of the tail and the malevolent beauty of the fin parting the surface. He'd never seen a shark in the water before.

Sally splashed him again, harder this time and the tail flicked, the fin accelerating quickly then slipping under the sea. As soon as it disappeared Jeff's reverie ended and fear hit him, first in the stomach, then in his throat. He wondered how long it had been there. If it was attracted by splashing. Stories flooded his head and he knew that whatever they do, they mustn't panic. Panicking would only invite an attack.

Unsure of her reaction and unwilling to risk it, he said nothing.

It surfaced again, on their right this time, cruising, and Jeff spotted it only in time to see it disappear. Sally was still laughing, waiting for him to splash back, but instead he held his hands in the air.

"You win," he said, "game over."

"No," she protested, "more!", splashing her hands on the surface, mimicking a spoilt little girl.

Jeff cringed. He wanted to see the fin. It was better if he knew where it was coming from.

"No," he said, "no more, I give up." It was like he was burning, every inch of him on fire waiting for it to happen. He began to swim silently toward her, but the idea of his white soles flashing in the water like two little fish was so consuming he had to stop and wade.

"Give me a hug, Sal," he said when he reached her.

"What?"

"Gimme a hug." Two bodies might be more intimidating than one. Behind her in the shallower water, near where he'd seen it initially, the fin surfaced again, closer this time. Circles, thought Jeff, concentric circles. He reached out and she put her arms around his neck, locking her legs about his waist, weighing nothing in the water.

"Ron'll be jealous if he sees us like this," she teased. "He'll think *we're* having an affair."

Jeff turned gently, keeping the shark behind her where he could see it, all the time edging them closer to shore. It was definitely moving faster now, the fin higher in the water.

"Na," he said, "he knows he's safe."

They'd almost completed a circle before it disappeared again and Jeff's stomach clenched. He took a big step toward shore but the water was still around his chest.

"Had enough?" he asked. It was hard to keep her eye and not look for the fin.

"Almost," she said, slipping off. "I'll race you."

"No, I'm too tired. Let's just walk." He guessed the shark would be behind them now and it was everything he could do to turn his back on it. In his mind's eye he could see the fin almost upon them.

"You've gone all quiet and vulnerable again," she said. "Are you thinking about her?"

"Something like that," he said.

In the waist-deep water he was aware of how sluggish and ungainly they were, so completely out of their element. The shark was making hunting circles. He could be leading them right into its path. Jeff risked a glance to his left but couldn't see anything. He took her hand and she slipped her arm around his waist, matching his stride. All he wanted to do was get to safety.

"It'll get better, you know," she said. "In time."

"Yeah, I know. Thanks, Sal."

It was on the right that he finally saw it again. First moving parallel, then suddenly turning to swim directly at them, fast. Jeff stiffened, watched it come for a few metres and then for no reason dart away, the fin sliding into the deep.

The water was splashing off their waists now and Jeff was at breaking point. Every step dragged and he tried to increase the pace. They were still deep enough for an attack. He wondered if he would have the courage to move, to pull her out of the way or even if he'd have the time.

When the water was thigh deep Jeff couldn't stand it any longer. He imagined the fin looming behind them, next to them, towering over them like Jaws about to destroy them.

"Run!" he urged suddenly. "Race you to the beach." He grabbed her wrist and half dragging her, thundered crashing through the shallows until they stood panting on the sand. Sally was giggling.

Glancing back there was nothing.

They walked up the beach hand in hand. Ahead, smiling broadly, Ron was waiting. Sally waved.

"How was that?" he asked, when they got to him. He was holding their towels.

"Lovely," answered Sally.

Jeff, saying nothing, looked over his shoulder at the sea again. He was shaking. "A bit cold," he said eventually.

When he turned to take his towel Ron was staring at him. For an instant they locked eyes. Quickly, almost imperceptibly, Ron shook his head then looked away. He had been watching all the time. He was part of it, too.

Sally and Ron lay under the umbrella while Jeff dried himself in the sun, his body still quivering. It seemed to take forever to get warm; his goosepimples resolute against the sun's rays as if he'd been frozen from the inside out. He couldn't shake it. In the end he slipped into his shoes and walked to the water's edge, the heaviness with him again.

When he got there, the shark was nowhere to be seen so he just stood for a while gazing at the blue. Presently he heard the crush of sand underfoot.

"Are you going to tell her?" It was Ron.

Jeff didn't move. The sun was in his eyes and he could feel another headache coming on.

The Politics of Fishing

The lodge owner was coming down for the weekend and Paul wanted to put on a good show. During the week he'd dug up two of the overgrown gardens, planted a row of lavender (getting horribly sunburnt in the process), cleaned up the area around the woodshed, weeded the fence-line, and finally on Friday, had mown the lawns. The lodge looked better than it had for a long time.

It was good of the owner to let him have the place. Newly separated and on the wrong end of a custody decision, Paul's life was, as he described it, 'shit at the moment'. He'd needed space and the owner, hearing of his desire to get out of the fast-lane, had offered him the place on the proviso that he clean it up. Paul was grateful and now he wanted to give the owner a good time.

On Friday evening, satisfied with his gardening efforts, Paul put his rod in the car and drove to a stream mouth he knew had been fishing well. The owner wouldn't be arriving until nine at the earliest and with the lodge clean and beer in the fridge, Paul had plenty of time to try and get a welcoming trout.

The stream mouth was always popular, not only because of its relative consistency, but also because of its proximity to a main highway. Recently, Paul had taken trout there and word had spread that the mouth was performing well. By the time Paul arrived, there were already six rods in the water.

He stepped into his waders, but as he prepared to take his usual position, two other fishermen walked in before him creating a barrier of men along the best part of lip. There was no room for another. Paul cursed softly. At times it was like fishing Grand Central Station.

Fishermen attracted fishermen, and often passing tourists, on seeing the line-up, would stop and enter the water themselves, assuming the great number of rods meant a great number of fish. Paul knew this wasn't always the case.

As was his habit, Paul dropped his flies in the water to see how they swam, then began to cast. It was difficult work. A covering of ominously low cloud blocked out the sun and a strong wind blew from behind, smothering his backcast, swirling the flies dangerously around him. When he was joined by other fisherman, safety dictated roll-casting, further increasing the difficulty he faced in getting his flies to the edge of the current. Then it began to rain.

For the next hour Paul fished the slack water in front of the current, occasionally risking a cast, the rain pummelling loudly against the hood of his jacket. By now there were eighteen people in the water. A row of fishermen standing up to their waists like the tree stumps of an old flooded bank. On almost every retrieve his sinking line would catch a reed bush that had been washed down the river into the mouth and twice he had lost flies. If there had been an alternative position in the line he would have moved, but even then, out of eighteen rods in the water there'd only been one fish taken — and that, from his spot closer to the rip.

In the end it was too much and just before dark, Paul gave in. Wet, irritated and without a fish, it was a long drive home.

Pulling into the driveway of the lodge and seeing the lights on, Paul realised the owner had already arrived. The owner didn't seem to mind that Paul hadn't been there to welcome him, but Paul felt bad. He was the host now.

Paul went to the fridge and took out the beers, and while he cooked dinner he filled the owner in on the state of the lodge, then, more importantly, on the fishing. The owner, while pleased with progress at the lodge, was more interested in the fishing, and when Paul told him that trophy-sized summer brown trout were being caught in the early mornings and around dark in the evenings, the owner was adamant that hunting browns was the thing to do. Between them they decided to rise early and go to a quiet stream mouth where Paul knew the browns would be.

At four-thirty they rose to the sound of driving rain. It must have rained all night, thought Paul. By now the river and mouth would be a dirty brown from the run-off and the fishing would be even harder. The owner didn't care. He didn't have a raincoat and he still didn't care. He didn't even want coffee.

But Paul had been right. Forty minutes later when they stood on the shore by the stream, the wind blew rain in their faces, the waves were up and the rip was unrecognisable. There was only one other person fishing.

"It's been blown to all hell," said Paul.

"It's still worth a try," said the owner, indicating the lone fisherman. "You never know."

They put on their waders and Paul showed the owner possible places to go. He had no raincoat, the wrong kind of line, but was determined to catch fish. Paul waded in above him and in the dim first light, watched the owner cast. They were long, tight loops that sliced through the wind. He was a good fisherman — better than Paul. If anyone caught fish today, it would be him.

Paul cast, letting his line drift across the rip as it sank. Almost immediately there was a strike. The owner looked back and seeing Paul's bending rod, gave a wave. It was a good omen.

Paul backed out of the current. He knew it was a slab. A long, skinny fish still recovering from its last effort of going up river to spawn. It was exhausted and had no fight in it. Paul brought it in gently. There were a lot of slabs around the mouths at this time of year, staying out of the main stream current, building up strength for their next spawning run. It was the period in their life when they were at their weakest and needed time to recover.

He got the trout to the beach and knelt beside it. It was a rainbow, but not much of one. It's flanks were drawn, and the usually colourful skin, lacklustre. Paul carefully extracted the hook and then stood away.

But the trout, even with it's tail in the water, was too tired to move. Paul put his rod down, placed his wet hands gently about the fish and moved it to deeper water until he felt the pull as it began to swim away.

He returned to his position and gave the thumbs down to the owner's enquiring glance. At least there were fish out there. The wind was blowing hard in his face, he couldn't be sure he was in the current properly and his cast was going everywhere, but there were fish.

Or so it seemed. For a long time after that they battled the elements without success until finally, further down the beach, the lone fisherman raised his rod and Paul watched it bend. Instantaneously, twenty metres away, a trout rose, writhing, crashing madly into the lake. The fisherman fought it carefully and when it was in the shallows he got his boot behind it and kicked it onto the sand. Paul knew then, that it was a fish worth keeping. Putting the boot in was the sign.

The owner gave Paul a look — as if he could do something and Paul shrugged.

They kept fishing and Paul took another slab. When it was on the beach the owner approached him.

"What fly are you using?" he asked. He had to shout because of the wind.

It was light now and Paul had abandoned the traditional black night-time patterns. Paul named the fly, but added, "Anything green. Green's good around here."

The owner nodded, made the change and shortly afterwards, hooked a slab. Paul was relieved to see the owner's rod finally bend. Even if it was a slab, at least he'd caught something. He watched as the owner hauled it contemptuously to the beach, but before he could land it, the fish spat the hook. The owner had been taking it too easy. Paul's heart sank. Beaten by a slab, what an insult.

The owner marched back into the water, casting furiously, but after that there was nothing for either of them. With the wind and rain and no browns about, it was an unpleasant morning.

Just as they were about to leave, Paul got a good strike. It was smaller fish but it fought well, jumping several times before he managed to control it. By the time he got to the beach to land it the owner was waiting for him.

"What do you think?" asked Paul.

"Looks good to me," said the owner.

Paul looked at the fish and considered the owner's lack of success.

"I think it's still a bit thin," he said.

"Maybe," said the owner.

Paul looked the fish over again, this time looking down on it from above the dorsal fin, checking its flanks. In other circumstances it might have been different.

"Another couple of months," he decided finally, "then she'll be dinner."

The owner didn't say anything.

Paul returned the fish to the water and they walked back to the car. The owner was wet through. Paul gave him a towel to dry himself and a polar-fleece to wear. Although it was the middle of summer and the wind wasn't cold, the owner was shaking. Paul kept the heater on all the way home.

When the owner emerged from the shower, Paul was cooking breakfast. "Three fish," he said. "It must be your lucky day."

"Na," said Paul. "You know slabs don't count."

But the owner didn't answer. Instead he pulled on the polar fleece and went outside to inspect the property and the work Paul had done.

Early that afternoon the owner suggested they take his boat out on a small lake nearby. It was well stocked and the owner had had much success there in the past. Paul agreed. He had little experience of this kind of fishing, but thought it would be the best chance the owner had of getting a decent fish. Over breakfast the owner had been decidedly short and had complained that work around the property wasn't going as fast as he'd expected. Paul hadn't known what to say. Agreeing to the lake seemed like the best solution.

But this too turned out to be a bad idea. It was windy and wet and cold in the little boat. The owner's outboard started to play up and against all odds Paul landed and released three more fish while the owner took nothing.

On the ride home the owner hardly spoke and Paul felt terrible.

That night, as Paul cooked dinner, the owner phoned his wife and reported the day's fishing. 'Six' and 'none' were all the words he used.

Paul didn't know what to do. There was little he could do about the weather or about his luck. He wanted the owner to catch fish, but short of not fishing himself couldn't think how to even the score.

In the morning they slept late, then lazed about reading newspapers and fishing books until the owner decided he was ready for something new. Paul had no idea where they should go. It was the middle of the morning. The weather had broken, the sun was blazing and it was now too hot for stream-mouth fishing.

Eventually the owner remembered a back-country pool high up on a local river that was sure to hold fish. It would require a long drive and an even longer bush walk, but the owner felt sure it would be worth it. He didn't know the trail exactly, he said, but felt sure they'd be able to find it.

It was a disaster. They drove for three-quarters of an hour up a dusty metal road, then tramped for an hour and a half through thick bush before admitting defeat. They couldn't even find the river let alone the pool. By the time they had walked out and driven back to the lodge they had wasted most of the day's fishing.

Now Paul was desperate. Soon the owner would have to leave and Paul would have failed. He didn't want the owner going home unhappy.

Although it was early, Paul suggested they fish the stream mouth he had tried so unsuccessfully on Friday night. The stream was on the owner's way home and it at least held the possibility of fish.

The owner concurred and taking his own car, followed Paul to the mouth. They assembled their rods, the owner duplicating Paul's fly combination, and entered the water together, quietly wading out to join the few locals already there.

With fewer people about this early in the evening, Paul had no trouble placing the owner in his favourite spot before surveying the water for himself. He wasn't too concerned where he went. All he wanted was for the owner to get a fish. For a minute he considered removing his flies, but in his heart knew that he couldn't stand leaving his line trailing pointlessly in the water. In the end, with the owner among the locals in the best position, Paul decided he had two options. Move down the line and try the slack water in front of the current as he had on Friday night or move up above everyone else into the unfashionable main rip. Paul chose the rip. It was colder and deeper than the edge Paul reasoned, and while unlikely to be holding fish, there was always a slim chance. It was all he needed to keep fishing.

He watched the owner casting his new shooting head, the line sailing gracefully forward into the water. Surely he would catch a fish this time.

One of the locals looked over at him. Paul knew him from before.

"How's the excitement?" asked Paul quietly.

"Slow," said the local. "Haven't touched a thing."

"Many taken?"

The local shook his head. On the other side of him Paul saw the owner was listening. Paul shrugged. It wasn't his fault the fishing was hard.

For three-quarters of an hour nothing happened. Nothing. People rarely spoke on the line and it was one of the reasons Paul liked fishing there so much. Because of the paradox of a collective solitude, being lost to yourself in the company of others. In the silence there was just the river, the lake and the fishing.

As he was apt to do on these occasions, Paul quickly drifted into his fishing state. A state in which he was unaware of time, barely thinking, only cast retrieve, cast retrieve, the repetitiveness of the action like a meditation.

When the fish hit it was as if he could feel the mouth close about the fly, feeling the touch before he knew the size. Raising his rod tip instinctively he felt the hook set, the fish turn and then the run. The retrieved line slid through his fingers so sharply, so desperately that he wondered if maybe he'd foul-hooked it. Then it was on the reel and it was still going. Finally, far in the distance it rose, arching its body, whipping head and tail. It was a big fish. Paul recovered some line but then the fish found the main channel and began to swim quickly toward him. He couldn't reel fast enough. The line went slack and Paul knew that without tension the fish would spit the fly. Paul swore at the fish. He reached up and by hand began hauling in line. Metres and metres of line. As soon as he had tension the fish turned and ran once more, again taking all the line. The reel sang. Paul palmed the spool to slow the fish's progress and the run stopped. He began to wind. The fish was tiring now and Paul kept it in the main channel where the depth kept it quiet. Eventually he began to back cautiously toward the shore.

"Might be one of them brownies," said the local, gently. Paul nodded. He got the fish behind the line of fishermen, across the shallow part of the stream mouth and in time, close enough to kick it onto the beach. It didn't want to come ashore, but Paul played it patiently until it tired enough for him to get the boot in.

With the trout safely on dry land, Paul reached into the front of his waders and extracted the priest. Aiming carefully he despatched the trout with three deliberate blows to the back of the head. Each blow made a satisfying thump. He removed the fly, then with a finger through the gills, washed the fish. Finally he sat down next to it and lit a cigarette.

It was beautiful. A brown trout. At nine pounds, the biggest he'd caught.

After a time he dug a trench in the wet sand and buried the fish, marking the place with a stick. As he resumed his place in the line the owner came over, congratulated him and borrowed a fly. Paul was embarrassed. He offered him the spot where he'd caught the fish, but the owner declined. It didn't matter anyway. They fished into dusk, but no one on the line had any success. Paul hardly noticed. The excitement of catching the fish still jangled through him.

Wading out of the river, Paul kept thinking about the owner. Not only had Paul caught all the fish, now he'd caught the prized fish. The one everyone wanted. But what else could he have done?

"Thanks" said the owner, as he prepared to leave. "It was enjoyable, if unproductive — for me anyway. It's definitely been your weekend."

"Yes," said Paul. "I've been lucky." He looked at the fish in his hand, then on impulse passed it to the owner. "It's too much for me," he said. "Have a dinner party."

The owner looked at the fish, then at Paul. "Are you sure?"

"Of course. I can't eat all that."

The owner nodded. "Okay then," he said. "Thanks. But you'll have to come too."

Paul hesitated. He had to go back some time. "Let me think about it," he said.

"Sure," said the owner.

They collapsed the rods and the owner got in his car. "Tuesday, would be a good day," he said.

"Right," said Paul.

Paul watched the car pull away. In the back was his fish. He leaned against a tree and lit another cigarette. Out in the stream mouth fishermen were lined up against the sunset, their long rods oscillating like metronomes. Paul thought about the owner driving home with his fish and laughed. He couldn't help it. Seven, zip. It had been a long time since he'd felt this good.

Dinner, he thought. Why not? It had been long enough. He felt ready for the city now, ready for the mainstream.

Breakages

Eventually he managed to haul himself out of the sofa and onto his feet. It was as if he'd broken free and finally he was standing. It was a good start, but now that he was up, he had to find a way out.

The room was a mess. The debris of life; books, CDs, pieces of clothing — some in boxes some out — lay strewn across the floor. Isolated patches of floorboards, islands in a sea of chaos, were the only thing left for him to pick a path to the door. And even they seemed impossible distances apart. Perhaps he shouldn't have bothered standing, but the same impulse that had left him stranded there for so long, now forced him out.

He didn't want to see her. Not anymore. Last night he had. At two o'clock in the morning, at three, and at four when the bed next to him was still empty, he had. Even after waking he'd wanted to; first stalking the tidier rooms, then depositing himself in the arms of the sofa to wait.

But now something had changed. Now it was as if, during his vigil, the emptiness of the bed had infiltrated his stomach and her absence had become a hunger, but one that had grown so strong, so painful that the mere thought of food made him feel sick. There was no way he could face her. When she returned it would be in her eyes and he didn't want to see it. If he waited any longer he would have to. No one can ever hide it completely.

It had been over for a while, he knew that, but he'd agreed to let her stay until she'd found a place. And over or not, nothing had prepared him for this. He'd had no idea it would hurt so much.

He looked across the floor and took a cautious first step. Stretching, right-foot-forward over a stack of old LPs, he planted a tentative boot between the printer and a glowing lava lamp, then moving quickly, fearful of losing his balance, pulled his left foot through and placed it on a pile of magazines. No sooner was it down than he was stuck, left foot in front, right foot behind like some sad imitation of Eros. He glanced about. Return was out of the question. So was any movement sideways. He refused to stand on the jacket he'd bought her and lacked any alternative site close by. Over-stretched between two points, there was little he could do but continue forward.

He raised his right foot and immediately, with sickening certainty, felt the connection. For milliseconds he froze, boot suspended hopefully at the place of contact as if this might reverse the action, but it didn't, and before the object hit the ground he knew it was the lava lamp. Off-balance, he continued through the step, stumbling now toward the safety of the hallway, hopping on and off patches of floor as if they were hot plates, stepping on the jacket's sleeve, knocking over a stack of books in the process.

Behind him the lamp toppled to the floor. When it hit, it cracked audibly, achingly audibly against the wood, the sound piercing him like a spear. He turned back and watched the clear water-like fluid drain from the cracked glass and pool around the lamp. They'd bought it together last winter, but now, after the division of goods, it was hers and he had broken it.

He stood in the hallway surveying the damage. There was little he could do. It was clearly beyond fixing and he doubted whether he wanted to risk the room again to clean it up. It was her own fault anyway. She shouldn't have left her packing half completed and the flat uninhabitable while she spent the night with someone else.

He turned to go, but the thoughts did not fully assuage his guilt. He remembered the day they had bought the lamp, she spotting it in a junk store window, under-valued, under-priced and ablaze, as if radiating warmth while they stood huddled in the cold. Without hesitation he had taken her hand, led her inside and paid the shop-keeper cash. That night she watched the heated globules rise and fall in the amniotic-like space as if mesmerised, finally insisting it be left on by their bedside so that she could watch it as they fell asleep.

He was still deciding what to do when he heard her key in the door. There was no panic, merely a sliding sensation as his plans of escape left him. When she entered he saw that she was dressed as she had been yesterday, jeans, T shirt, jacket, but that her hair was still wet from the shower and there was no longer any make-up on her face. She looked surprised to see him.

"Hello," she said.

"Hi." He thought he heard the sound of a car driving away. He moved to his right and she stepped past him in the hallway. His hand was on the door knob when she saw it.

"You arsehole," she said softly. "You broke my lava lamp. You complete and utter arsehole."

He walked back to where she was standing to look at the lamp. The remnants of the clear fluid were still there, but now the viscous red inner had seeped out of the lamp and lay in thick rivulets around it on the floor.

"How could you?" she asked.

He didn't answer. There was nothing to say.

I was Mr New Zealand
or
What Scares Me

Shortly after the mail arrives I make for the shed, slamming the door, shutting out the din as over the fence he pushes the mower through three months of thick, damp grass. I fall into my chair and in the darkness, battle the tears. I'm shaking.

In 1959 it wasn't going to be like this. Then beer was three and six a jug, Capstans a couple of bob a packet and I had a future. I was somebody.

I stand, turn on the light and cut a new strip of sandpaper for the block. At the workbench I touch the wood gently, then begin; forward, backward . . . calming myself; breathing in the macrocarpa. Slowly time fades. My eyes dry, the drone of the mower vanishes. After a while it's almost as if the letters never arrived.

Almost.

When I step out of the shed and walk back to the house, it's already late in the afternoon. He's finally stopped mowing. Now they're on the lawn discussing the alterations again, desperate to start changing things.

I get the kettle on, and, ignoring the letter that sent me to the shed, re-read the other. I should be flattered.

Dear Former Mr. New Zealand, it begins... then a personal salutation, *Jack,* In celebration of . . . and in light of your valued . . . we would be honoured if you would present the prestigious Mr New Zealand 1999: Millennium Award, making a short speech and . . .

119

Thirty years late and they want a speech too. I can't help but laugh. Inside the envelope is an RSVP card. They must be crazy.

I drop the whole lot on the bench, pour boiling water into the teapot, cosy it, and go back into the garden for some dinner vegetables.

It's ridiculous.

When the new bloke from next door calls out, I'm on my knees digging potatoes. I look up to see him straining over the fence, just the top of his head visible. With his hands on either side he looks like a 'Kilroy was here' cartoon.

"Hello," he says.

I give him a nod and a grunt.

"We couldn't help noticing your garden and thought you might like some grass clippings for compost."

It's an educated voice, a lawyer or something. I nod and put my hand up to answer, but he waves me away. "No, you stay there. We'll bring some round."

Within minutes he and the girl are in the driveway pushing a huge, precariously balanced mound of grass in a wheelbarrow.

"Where to?" he asks, but spotting the composter, marches past and dumps the load at its base.

"Bryce," he says as they return, "Bryce Jackson, and Anna, my wife."

I shake their hands and give him the note I've written. *Jack Cattley. Can't speak.* I tap the patch on my throat with my pen and squeeze out the best sort of greeting I can, somewhere between a grunt and a squawk.

"We sort of guessed," she says.

I take the pad I keep in my pocket and scrawl out another.

"Some vegetables would be lovely," she answers. She is short with a strong frame, legs like an Edwardian piano and a smile that would charm the Irish. He is skinny, like he's never done a lick of exercise in his life. "Can I help?" she asks, but I shake my head.

Regardless, she takes the supermarket bag and holds it open while I get them some potatoes and a couple of lettuces.

"You're too generous." she says. "You must come for dinner so we can share them." She seems genuine, but we know what a strained meal that would be. I smile noncommittally.

They turn down the driveway and I go back to the veges. Suddenly the place seems very quiet. Just the shadows and the lawn and the veges and the flowers and me. Somewhere down the street, kids are playing.

I go back inside, give the teapot a few turns, then start again. It's stewed.

At six-thirty sharp, Anna arrives on my doorstep and suddenly I am a dinner guest. It's the first time I've been in this house since the eighties, I think. Little has changed, but their furniture, all modern and stylish, looks out of place against Edna's old carpet.

They put me in an easy chair with a glass of beer and Anna goes into the kitchen. I am still in my everyday clothes and back in my sink two potatoes await the pot.

Immediately Bryce takes charge of the conversation. Sitting over a newspaper he relates to us amusing anecdotes, explaining so that neither Anna nor I need answer. He tells us first about a bungled bank robbery, and about an Italian gigolo who, paid in shoes, died with five hundred pairs in his apartment. Then laughing, he tells us about a circus dwarf who bounced off a trampoline into the mouth of a hippopotamus. By the time he gets to the fish there are already tears in his eyes.

Apparently, he says, someone right in our city, is sending dead fish to politicians. A protest against environmental damage caused by polluted storm water run-off. They collect rotting fish from the beach, vacuum pack them, then send them in bubble-wrap envelopes to culpable authorities.

At the beginning it's not that funny, but by the end Bryce is laughing so hard he's set me off too, grinning stupidly, all teeth and gums and staccato rasps as we imagine politicians opening envelopes of dead fish. It's good. We hit the table and rock together, and suddenly I've got tears in my eyes. The laughter chokes up and I want to tell him about all the hours *I* spent fishing in that harbour, about the fish *I* pulled out and about how, being out on the water was the one thing I loved more than anything, even the gym. Instead, while Bryce keeps laughing, I take my handkerchief and pretend to wipe away the joy, smiling, hoping they can't tell the difference. Shortly afterwards Anna calls us to the table, Bryce pours wine and we begin.

At the start of the meal they talk at me — giving out information like headlines: they have taken two weeks holiday to settle in; she is a banker, he an accountant; they are going to renovate the entire house; Bryce will do the work; they plan to have a family here.

Later, information exhausted, their conversation becomes a game of charades.

You're a widower. Shake. *Never married?* Nod. *Lived here most of your life.* Nod. *You're a butcher* ...demonstrate again . . . *oh, a builder!* Double nod, squeeze out a noise.

It's only after dinner, on our second brandy, that they ask me something that might require more than a head movement. I pull out the pen.

Too many cigarettes, I scrawl. Then to another; *on the waiting list.*

I don't mind. They're good company. She is bright and forthright and reminds me of girls I never married. He is quieter, more serious.

At the end of the evening it's Bryce who walks me to the gate.

⟨≳⋙⋘≲⟩

On my way to the shed the next morning, they are outside on their patio. Bryce waves the morning paper.

"Another one," he guffaws triumphantly through the fence. "Another fish!" I give him a wave and a grin, but keep going.

Inside the shed the air is still, thick with the smell of wood and resin. From my pocket I take yesterday's letter and place it with the others. Bugger them.

Usually this is when I work the hardest, but today, tired after last night's drinking, I don't feel like it. Instead in the half-light of the dirty window, I walk around my nearly completed project, run my hand over its lines, feel the flow of its curves, then sink into the old armchair and stare at it.

Of all the things I have built in this shed, it will be the most beautiful. God willing, it will carry me to places I've only dreamed about, or, if I've made a mistake, nowhere at all.

I settle back into the chair and feel myself begin to doze. I don't fight it. Occasionally I broach consciousness, and their voices, like children at play, drift across to me. This time he's done something wrong, that time they're laughing.

If it were to be now, here, this would be a nice way.

⋘⋙

A few days later Anna comes by to invite me over for dinner again. In the hallway she spots the photograph and suddenly I'm being interrogated. I give in, show her the album and, as a joke, the invitation to speak. She doesn't laugh. Instead she immediately tries to convince me to go, that it would be good for me, and I rue the fact that I can't clearly explain to her how long ago those days were. How anything I did has long been forgotten, or anything I had to offer since, ignored. The millennium, like it or not, is a young person's party. A party for those with a future.

But she is persistent, and even if I had the words, wouldn't listen. It's only when I write a quick, bold *NO!* on the pad that she drops it, holding up her hands in mock defeat and falling silent.

We are almost at their house before she tries the only question missed last night.

"Jack . . ." she asks. "What is it that you do in the shed, every day?"

I shake my head, shrug 'nothing', but she's not having it.

"Come on," she says, "it can't be that much of a secret."

I stop walking, turn, look her square in the eye, then winking, tap the side of my nose.

"God!," she exclaims. "You're impossible!"

⋘⋙

123

We sit under the awning playing chess. Bryce is back at work, but Anna still has days up her sleeve. She's supposed to be stripping wallpaper, but each day comes over to be fleeced by me.

This morning it's her own fault. She's not concentrating; still intent on getting me to the awards. She's tried everything.

I make another move and Anna sits forward to observe. She stays there, back straight, poised like a pointer dog, but doesn't respond. Seconds pass.

"Let's go for a walk," she says suddenly.

I look up. To date our friendship hasn't exceeded the boundaries of our houses.

"Come on," she says standing. "It'll make a nice change."

Inside the car the radio is tuned to a classical station. I tap her arm. *Where to?*

"It's a surprise," she says.

We drive through the local shops, past subdivisions and the houses I built, past the gym, and finally, with a left turn, to the beach. The tide is out and she leads us down to the packed wet sand where the walking is easier. There's a slight wind blowing and I'm glad for my jacket. We've only walked a short distance when I stop her and point out a dead fish with the toe of my shoe.

"Yeagh," she says. Then with a laugh. "Maybe we should take it home for Bryce."

Why here? I sign.

"It was in the photo album. You won your first title here. A beach competition."

"Ppp," is the best I can manage.

"You wouldn't have to make a speech, you know. And you'd get to see some of your mates from around the country again."

I shake my head adamantly. I don't need to be reminded what I once was.

"Come on, Jack. I'll go with you. No speech, no handing over anything and I'll be there." She's got the same crease in her forehead she gets when playing chess.

Down the beach a car's stuck in the sand.

She breaks into a smile and pulls from her pocket the RSVP envelope. "Tick the box, Jack," she says.

You'll come?

"Promise," she says.

I tick the box, then with a doubtful shake, seal it shut.

"Well done," she says. She takes me by the arm and smiling, leads me off in search of a post box. Checkmate.

⋘⋙

As soon as the mail arrives, I forget that I am expecting Anna. Instead I go straight to the shed. There I take the letter and angrily pin it to the wall alongside the others.

My wallpaper. Pictures of Mr New Zealand and next to them official correspondence advising of his position at the wrong end of a queue — even though he's been around longer than most. This time, thanks to another health system reshuffle, he's been postponed.

They didn't tell us it would be like this. Just like they didn't tell us about the tar when we bought the fags or privatisation when we paid our taxes. They didn't tell us about being forgotten.

It was the same for my old man. He died like this too, except his was in his gut and he was ten years younger. It made him cry. A fifty-eight year old who'd hunted wild boar with nothing but a long-bladed knife driven to desperation by the humiliation of illness. Having to be helped to shit by his son. I remember his hands, gnarled like Kauri trunks, bunching to wipe his eyes. Tears of frustration and helplessness spilling out as everything failed; his body, his mind, his self-control.

And now they're going to let it happen to me.

"Jack? Jack are you in there?"

Outside Anna has come looking.

I stay shtumm, but the door cracks open and she takes a breath. She only opens the door as wide as her body, but instead of entering she just stands in the doorway staring, following the light across the floor and onto the walls. Finally her eye falls on me.

"Can I come in?" she says. I barely nod. Now they'll both know.

She eases quietly through the door and goes first to the letter-clad wall, reading the correspondence, then looks at the trophies and photographs and clippings mounted next to them.

She doesn't speak, instead she turns to the work-bench in the centre of the room. Without trying to touch it she circuits it, giving it her complete attention like she's in an art gallery.

Finally, she turns to me.

"Beautiful coffin," she says.

Early evening there's a knock on the door. Before I'm out of my chair I know who it is. No one else has knocked on that door for years, apart from collectors.

"G'day Jack," says Bryce. He looks sheepish, like a kid come to collect an errant ball. "Hope I'm not bothering you." I shake my head. Over my shoulder the tv's on. "Anna and I were wondering if you'd like to come to dinner tonight. She's cooking a roast."

I shake my head.

I know what they're doing and I don't need it. I'll be fine.

"The thing is," he says, scratching his neck, "Anna says that if I don't bring you, she'll come over and get you herself."

We look at each other, widen our eyes, then burst out laughing.

I put on a clean shirt and get my jacket.

⬦⬦⬦

"The Prime Minister *and* the Minister of Fisheries," says Bryce a couple of days later, laughing. I take the tape-measure, measure again, mark the spot and have him drive in the peg. "Both of them got one. And they still don't know who's doing it. I bet it's driving them wild."

I measure again, show him the place for the next peg and he hammers it in. "The thing is what to do when they catch them? What can you do to a public icon? Everyone's on their side." He's standing on the string, and when I tug at it he stumbles trying to get off. "Sorry," he says. He stands about awkwardly waiting for me to show him the position of the next peg. He's thinking. About fish probably.

"Thanks again for helping me with this deck, Jack," he says suddenly. "I don't know what I would have done without you."

I don't bother looking up, but point to the next place with the tape measure.

❧

We never talk about it. Not once. We don't even talk about the waiting list. The closest we get is Anna getting a bit teary-eyed one evening and telling us how much she misses her Dad and how she wishes she'd been in the country. Then it's like it never happened. I help Bryce with his deck and suddenly become 'construction consultant' as Anna calls it. Around there every day showing him what to do and what not to do. Getting him to hire tradesmen when needed.

At some point there's yet another reshuffle. When that letter arrives, no one bats an eye-lid. "Another speaking engagement" is all Anna can say.

❧

When the taxi sounds its horn, there's a funeral pyre burning in my backyard, complete except for me. In the concrete block incinerator, the coffin, doused in petrol and broken into kindling, flames, a pillar of smoke rising into the still evening air. Entombed with the coffin are the black and white photographs of a past life. As are the letters. There's to be no more waiting. I'm getting a voice. It's only coincidence the operation's the same day as the awards.

Bryce escorts me from the front door to the roadside where Anna and the taxi are waiting. Anna hugs me and I climb in.

"We'll come and see you," she says. I nod, though for a two-night stay there's no need. She takes Bryce's hand. As the taxi driver releases the hand-brake tears form in her eyes.

"Hurry home, Jack" she says.

I give her my best smile.

Of course, I will, I want to say. *Of course, I will. I have to. Otherwise, who'll send all the fish?*